For more than forty years,
Yearling has been the leading name
in classic and award-winning literature
for young readers.

Yearling books feature children's
favorite authors and characters,
providing dynamic stories of adventure,
humor, history, mystery, and fantasy.

Trust Yearling paperbacks to entertain,
inspire, and promote the love of reading
in all children.

## OTHER YEARLING BOOKS YOU WILL ENJOY

# Mike Stellar: Nerves of STEEL

### K. A. Holt

A YEARLING BOOK

This is a work of fiction. Names, characters, places, and incidents either are the product of the author's imagination or are used fictitiously. Any resemblance to actual persons, living or dead, events, or locales is entirely coincidental.

Visit us on the Web! www.randomhouse.com/kids

Educators and librarians, for a variety of teaching tools, visit us at www.randomhouse.com/teachers

The Library of Congress has cataloged the hardcover edition of this work as follows:
Holt, K. A.
Mike Stellar : nerves of steel / K. A. Holt.
p. cm.
Summary: Mike is suspicious when his family joins an expedition to Mars at the last minute, and his fears are confirmed when all of the adults on the colonizing mission, including his parents, begin to act strangely.
ISBN 978-0-375-84556-7 (trade) — ISBN 978-0-375-94556-4 (lib. bdg.) — ISBN 978-0-375-85385-2 (e-book)
[1. Planets—Environmental engineering—Fiction. 2. Space flight to Mars—Fiction.
3. Cyborgs—Fiction. 4. Space colonies—Fiction. 5. Family life—Fiction.
6. Science fiction.] I. Title.
PZ7.H7402Mik 2009
[Fic]—dc22
2008027272

ISBN 978-0-375-84557-4 (pbk.)

Printed in the United States of America

10 9 8 7 6 5 4 3

First Yearling Edition

To Steven, Sam, Georgia, and Isaac—
my favorite space cadets

# Mike Stellar:
## Nerves of
# STEEL

Mike Stellar
Mrs. Halebopp, English
May 31, 2174

## The Process Of Terraforming, Made Simple

Don't capitalize "of."

So here's what they do: The Project sends exploration

This is not a proper introduction, Mike.

crews out to search for ice. And when I say out to

search for it, I don't just mean out to the Plug 'n' Sip to

find a bag of ice. It'd have to be a honkin' big bag of

ice, because it would have to cover part of a PLANET.

That's what the crazy Project dudes want. Ice on a

"Honkin' big"? "Crazy Project dudes"? This is a research paper on terraforming, Mike, not a paper on twenty-first-century rap songs.

planet. So they can melt it. So how do they melt it?

STOP beginning sentences with "so."

With gigantic mirrors! In space! That look kind of like

While I appreciate your enthusiasm, none of those sentences are complete.

sails on old-fashioned ships! The mirror-sails can

range anywhere from five miles across to two hun-

dred miles across, can you believe that?!

Please, no editorializing, Mike.

Once the space crews are finished building the

mirror-sails (sometimes this takes years and years),

they glide the gigantic mirror-sails over the ice on the

planet and then turn the sails toward the sun. Why do

they do that, you ask? Well, I'll tell you. The sails

Do not be smart-alecky.

reflect the sun's heat down onto the ice and melt it.

My dad showed me how this works by taking a mag-

nifying glass outside and using it to melt an ice cube.

2

It's more fun to fry ants this way, so I wonder if maybe

*Stay on topic. Avoid first person.*

the mirror-sails could be used to fry aliens. Anyway,

the ice starts to melt and that releases carbon dioxide

into the air. Carbon dioxide is the stuff humans spew

*"Spew"?*

out when they breathe. This helps to heat the planet

up somehow. Once the planet heats up and the water

*Somehow? More details, please.*

melts, it's easy to start growing plants and grasses

and things like that. That's when the fast-growing

plants and frankenbugs and bacteria and stuff are

*"Frankenbugs" is slang. Please use the proper term.*

dropped onto the plnet. Then, a few years later—

*You have spelled "planet" incorrectly.*

voilà—Earth II (or III or IV). The whole process is called

terraforming. Some people are really against it, like

my sister, Nita. But other people think it's just great. I

don't really care one way or another.

*Lose the last three, editorializing sentences.*

3

All in all, a much better report than last time, Mike. You have to stop with the editorial comments, though, and you MUST START USING PROPER PARAGRAPHS. Research reports are serious work. You are presenting facts. Please keep that in mind when you rewrite this paper. (And don't be discouraged, Mike. This will make a decent ten-minute speech due NEXT MONTH.)

C+

"Rewrite? Ten-minute speech? *Arrgh*. I knew Mrs. Halebopp was out to get me." I marched over to a tree, thought about kicking it, and stomped on the ground instead.

"Her giant head blocks out the sun and her black-hole eyes read my mind. I know they do." I shook my report at my friend Stinky for emphasis. "It already took me like eight million years to research this paper, now I have to do it again? And read it in front of people? I am toast."

Stinky stared with his mouth kind of open. I'm not usually a stomping and yelling kind of kid.

"Worse than toast," I continued, my voice cracking, making me madder. "I'm oily, melted margarine dripping off of toast and onto the floor. I'll be smeared into the carpet at school. Forever. No escape."

I crumpled up the cellopage printout of my report

and threw it into an ant bed I'd been nudging with my foot. The ants streamed over it, seething, taking out their frustration on my 100 percent recyclable, 100 percent doomed report.

"Mike?" Stinky gawked as if my head had exploded. "You need to seriously cut back on the drama."

Stinky was always saying that. I could be on fire, with robots eating my legs, and he'd be all, "Calm down, man. Things'll be fiiiine." It was funny, because just looking at him, you'd think Stinky would be the opposite. His hair stood up like his mom must've accidentally electrocuted him when he was a baby. His arms were splotchy with freckles; his laugh sounded like a machine gun. He seemed like the human embodiment of the word "staccato." And yet he was as calm as the wake of a Dirigible Cruiser.

He was silly and fun and, well, not actually very stinky. But he'd been my friend since we were both in diapers, and I didn't care that people still jokingly held their noses whenever he walked by. (You accidentally drop air-freshener tablets into the boys' room toilets *instead of the stink bombs you promised,* and apparently, you never live down everyone's disappointment.)

Stinky was my best friend and I listened to him . . . most of the time. So I sat down on the ground (away from the ants) and put my face in my hands.

"You need to just relax. Mrs. Halebopp, she's not the devil. I mean, she did give you a C+. That's a hundred times better than your astrophysics report."

I winced. I still didn't know anything about astrophysics.

"Thanks," I said.

Stinky punched me on the shoulder. My mouth curled into a tiny O. If only he punched as carefully as he chose his stink bombs.

"Your paper isn't that bad, Mike. I know you feel this pressure or whatever 'cause your mom and dad are big shots over at the Project, but I don't think Mrs. Halebopp cares about that. She might not even know about it."

*"Ha!"* I said, rubbing my face and my hair. I smelled my hands. Shampoo, head grease, humiliation . . . yep . . . that was me, all right.

"Everyone knows who my parents are, dude. Especially after . . . you know . . ."

"Well, think of it this way . . . after that disaster, she probably thinks you're not very smart at all, and she's cutting you some slack. Heck. I want some slack cut for me. Just 'cause your parents kil—"

I jumped up.

"Are you trying to make me feel better, Stink? 'Cause it's not working." I couldn't believe he'd almost said what he'd almost said. Stinky of all people. He *never* said anything about my parents, not even when

Hubble was lost. I was really mad now. All my day's frustrations were burning right between my eyes. It made me squint and frown and bite the inside of my cheek. I rubbed my palms on the front of my new solar pants—pants that Stinky, who I thought was my *friend*, helped me pick out at the mall last week.

"What are you trying to say, *Yeager*?" I growled, using his real name, which I knew he loathed. I marched over to where he stood. "Are you saying my parents are stupid, just like me? They killed a bunch of innocent people 'cause they're so dumb?"

Stinky looked surprised and put his hands in the air like I was holding a particle gun on him.

"No, Mike. I . . . I was trying to make you feel better!"

"Better? Accusing my parents of . . ." I trailed off. The area around us suddenly darkened and I caught a whiff of burnt coffee beans.

Mrs. Halebopp.

Her beehive hairdo towered over us, leaning forward off of her Jupiter-sized head.

"Is there trouble here, boys?" she asked through pursed lips, sunlight struggling to seep through her big blue hair. "Do I need to involve Mr. Burton?"

"Uh . . . ," I said.

"Uh . . . ," Stinky repeated. Our last involvement with the principal had left us both with three days of detention.

"I didn't think so," she said grouchily, leaning in closer to me so that I could nearly taste the burnt coffee smell reeking from her polka-dot shirt. "Don't let me catch you misbehaving, Mr. Stellar." She thrust a fat old-fashioned book into my hand. It weighed about a frillion pounds. I stumbled forward a bit, dangerously close to actually . . . *touching* . . . Mrs. Halebopp. "You don't have time to waste now that your speech is due next week instead of next month." She stepped back with what seemed to be a gleeful look on her face. Or maybe she was just grimacing in the sunlight.

"But," I said, "I . . ."

"And let's hope you deliver your speech with more eloquence than your current rhetoric." She pointed an extra-long, creaky-looking finger at me. "Use that book to research your paper. Kids these days need to learn that there's nothing wrong with doing things the old-fashioned way." After a moment she turned on her heel and walked briskly back to the classroom.

I stuffed the thousand-pound book into my bag. It was eerily quiet as Stinky and I continued to stare daggers at each other. Usually you could at least hear the flag clanging against the flagpole. I looked ahead. The new flag was "waving" in the distance. It was a holo-gram installed by the PTA (a "weatherproof flag that shines day and night") and it gave me the creeps. I couldn't believe I was thinking it, but maybe Mrs.

Halebopp was right. Sometimes old-fashioned things *are* better.

I gave Stinky one last dirty look and stomped down the sidewalk toward home. I could hear him yelling, "Mike! Are we still airboarding at Jones Park this weekend? Mi-ike!" after me, but I didn't turn around.

As I walked home grumbling, I did have one slightly happy thought. It was Thursday. That meant *MonsterMetalMachines*. My favorite show: Fierce Mangle and Preditator duking it out in three dimensions all over the living room. I had to pick up the pace and make it home soon. Otherwise my sister, Nita, would snag the remote and force me into watching some cruddy Earthlings for Earth propaganda. That would be just my luck—stuck with Neeters and her crazy-boring brainwashing shows all night.

I looked at the sky, wishing this day would hurry up, when I heard a buzzy, mechanical whir behind me.

I recognized the sound immediately. Mom's electri-car. The window slid down and Mom said, "Hey there, Mr. Man." (She always calls me Mr. Man. All I can say is: *So. Dorky.*)

"Um, hi." I rolled my eyes.

"Nice greeting." She let the electri-car roll to a stop. "You want to hop in and explain why you're running so late?"

"Okay."

Mom smiled her big ol' mysterious smiley smile and said, "Window." The window buzzed up. Then the passenger door slid open and I hopped into the electri-car. I tossed my bag into the backseat and said, "Belt." The seat belt slid out from the sides of the seat, crushing the waistband on my solar pants and probably ruining their charging ability forever. I tugged at it a little. Mom's e.c. always had extra-tight seat belts.

"Why so late?" she asked again.

I scratched an ant bite on my toe. "It's a long story."

"How about a five-minute version?" Mom was trying not to sound mad, but her voice had that . . . *tone.*

I pulled my Star City Quarks baseball cap down over my face. "I had a detention," I said from under my cap, flinching with the anticipation of Mom's reaction.

Mom gasped. "Michael! Another one? What is the deal, kid? Why are you getting in so much trouble these days?"

As if she didn't know.

I shrugged and hid under the dark red interior of my cap.

"So?" Mom asked, reaching over and flicking my cap off my face.

I stared out the window. Only a few hours earlier, Stinky and I were in detention together and still best friends. Now I could just wring his—

"Michael!"

"What?"

"What happened?"

"I, uh . . ." I totally spaced out on what we were talking about. I was staring at my reflection in the window.

Dark brown wavy hair like Mom's, only shorter. Brown eyes with flecks of purple, like Dad's. A long nose. (Dad calls it a Roman nose. Stinky calls it a schnoz.) A pointy chin like Gram's. Five or six freckles that could almost be connected to form Orion's Belt on my left cheek. I looked like a normal kid. But inside I felt like a volcano. Fiery one minute, quiet the next, and then back to fiery again. I sighed, expecting steam to come shooting out of my nose.

Squaring my jaw, I grimaced at myself in the window, working on an angry yet forgiving expression to give Stinky when he got on his knees and apologized—

"To get a detention, Michael. *Come on*. This is the five-minute version, not five hours." Mom engaged the e.c.'s autodrive and turned in her seat to stare at me. Her eyebrows squinched in a menacing V shape.

"Right," I said, reaching for my hat to hide behind again. "I, uh, creamed Marcy Fartsy with a dodgeball. In gym class. During a time-out."

"Michael Newton Stellar!"

I could see it coming a mile away—the excuse to holler at me. I beat her to the punch and hollered, "She started it! She said you and Dad . . ." I tugged on my cap. "She started it." Now my eyebrows became menacing.

"So that's why you were late? There wasn't anything else? Say, an after-detention meeting with Mrs. Halebopp about your terraforming report?"

"Huh? How did—?"

"Mrs. Halebopp called me. She said you're not serious about your schoolwork anymore."

"I'm serious about my schoolwork!" I yelled, knowing full well I wasn't serious about it at all.

The electri-car bumped over the recognition pod in the drivedropper of our small moon-stucco house. (Supposedly moon-stucco has actual moondust in it from the mining trips years ago. Dad says that's all bunk. They just add some sparkly silica to regular ol' stucco. I kind of like the idea of having pieces of the moon on my house, though, so I ignore Dad.)

"Right," said Mom. I could tell she was trying to regulate her irritation. "We've talked about what to do when the other kids tease you, Mike, and we've talked about your study habits. Am I going to have to take away your flight sims?"

"Aw, Mom. Sim games have nothing to do with how boring school is. Plus, I'm really *good* at the sims. What if I want to be a pilot one day?"

"You don't get to be a pilot if you spend all your time playing video games and hacking into your sister's com-bracelets. You have to apply yourself, Mike. Study. Use those smarts of yours for good, not evil."

I let a small smile escape. Mom knows that Fierce Mangle is my favorite MonsterMetalMachine, and it's funny when she tries to imitate his robotic tone. "Use. Those. Smarts. For. Gud. Not. Eee. Vile."

"Just get out of the e.c. We'll talk about it later," Mom said.

I said, "Belt," and my seat belt snapped undone. I grabbed my bag, said, "Door," and hopped out of the electri-car.

Mom gathered her work stuff and we headed up the front walk while she clicked the button on her key chain. The drivedropper gobbled up the electri-car and stored it under the house.

I stomped up the walk ahead of Mom, imagining the impending talk she and I—and Dad—were going to have. As the words "grounded," and "big trouble," and "no sims for a month" ran through my head rather loudly, I flung open the door and crashed headfirst into Nita.

"Ahh! You freak, get off!" Nita yelled, staggering backward under the weight of my flailing body.

"Get your fat head out of my way and I won't have to stomp on it," I said, still off balance.

"Oh, children," said Mom, sidestepping our melee. "Why can't my babies just get along?"

Nita made a noise like she was trying to cough up a hair ball and she walked toward the stairs. I tossed my bag on the hallway table and headed toward the visera-tor room.

Mom kicked off her shoes and rubbed her face. "Nita? Honey? Is Daddy home?"

From the foot of the stairs, Nita said, "He's in the study reading all the latest news about your evil project." She turned off the light over the staircase, muttered something about saving energy, and marched her big butt up to her room. She passed Dad as he came down.

Dad was wearing his readers and the walls reflected them as he came down the stairs. They shone on the wall in a distorted font. *Historical! Brave!*

Mom went up and kissed him on the neck.

"Howdy, little lady."

"Ugh," I moaned. "There's a *kid* in the room, you guys." I grabbed the remote and flipped on the viserator. It shot whorls of three-dimensional static through the room.

"Man," I grumbled. "Someone really needs to fix this thing. It's been shooting static like this for ages." Mom and Dad briefly looked over at me and stared at the static.

"Hey, what's this?" Dad asked suddenly. I twisted around on the sofa. The fat book from Mrs. H had slid out of my bag onto the table. The fingerbulbs of his readers clattered as he clumsily picked it up and tried to flip through it. "This book is fantastic. Look at the binding." He held the book up like it was a newborn baby. "Where did you get this old girl?"

I made a face. "From another old girl. Mrs. Halebopp gave it to me to help research a report I'm writing."

"Well, wasn't that nice?" Dad said absently. "Mind if I take a look? I'll get it back to you soon."

I shrugged and turned around to watch the vis. Dad's new love affair with old-fashioned books was nerdy. At least he still used his readers for news. It seemed like lately he was always in his study, staring into his palms as the fingerbulbs flashed the day's headlines over and over.

The static whorls finally disappeared and a three-dimensional commercial appeared.

A guy was standing in a yard with weeds up to his knees, and his hands on his head. An announcer's voice boomed, "—latest technology! Just grasp the grasshrinker and throw directly on your yard. In minutes the grass will shrink to a well-manicured size!"

*Stupid grasshrinkers,* I thought. I was supposed to shrink the lawn last weekend but I forgot. I quickly flipped the channel, hoping Dad wouldn't hear and lecture me. I flipped and flipped, trying to find *MonsterMetalMachines,* and it suddenly hit me that my show wasn't going to be on. Every channel was full of news about Liftoff Day tomorrow. I had totally forgotten about it. Blah.

Dad sat next to me.

"Exciting stuff!" he said with a big smile. He looked happier than I had seen him in a long time.

"Yeah," I said. Mom sat down on my other side.

"Michael," she said, glancing at Dad, "there's something your father and I would like to talk to you about."

Dad took the remote and turned off the viserator.

Yuh-oh.

Turning the viserator off always meant trouble. And whenever Mom said "your father and I," that really meant something not good was about to happen. I knew that car ride home had gone too easy.

"Would you please run upstairs and get Nita?" she asked.

Interesting. Usually Nita wasn't involved in my getting into trouble. Especially lately. She never got into trouble at all anymore. It was like she had discovered parental hypnosis that let her be nasty and get away with it.

I halfheartedly banged the intercom, hoping it would work so I wouldn't have to go all the way upstairs. It was all staticky. Stupid thing had been broken for months. Mom used to be right on top of fixing stuff like that, but lately she was all work, work, work.

I sighed and climbed the stairs. As I reached her room, I gleefully anticipated Nita's finally getting yelled at—even if it meant my getting yelled at, too.

"Neeters. Mom and Dad want you downstairs," I yelled at her closed door. She had a poster on it that said "Earthlings for Earth." The letters were made of contorted people lying in a field of green grass.

"Go away, freak."

"Okay. But they want you downstairs," I said, giving her door a bang. She made me so mad. I hated that she hated me. But I couldn't do anything about it except pretend that I hated her back.

I went downstairs and I heard her door open. I slowly walked back into the living room, like an animal led to slaughter. I mentally prepared my usual defense: raising my eyebrows and frowning in confused "who, me?" irritation.

Mom ran her hands through her hair and Dad tried to nibble on his fingernails but finally noticed he still had on his readers. The word "amazing" reflected on his left cheek.

I laughed nervously and said, "You're amazing, Dad." Then he took the readers off one fingerbulb at a time, flashing words everywhere. Most people turn off their readers before they remove them, but not Dad. Nita plopped down next to Mom and glowered at the floor.

"Well, kids," Mom said as Dad's left-hand reader rolled across the coffee table and flashed "dangerous" diagonally on the wall, "there's no sense in beating around the bush."

She paused and Dad took her hand.

I shot Nita a look that said, "What kind of trouble have you gotten me into?" Nita shot me a look that said, "Shut it. I'm concentrating hard on preparing the biggest hair ball noise I've ever made."

Mom smiled and squeezed Dad's hand.

"Kids, we're moving to Mars."

There was a pause as Nita and I sucked all the air out of the room.

"Tomorrow."

I heard a thump and looked around. Surprisingly, it had come from me.

I had fallen off the sofa.

3

"**With parades, celebrations,** and a certain amount of apprehension, Liftoff Day has arrived. A full two years after the ill-fated Mars Expedition and the loss of the *Spirit,* the Star City–based Project is ready to try again.

" 'We feel infinitely confident,' states the Project president, Aurora Hazelwood. 'Watch out, Mars, here we come.' "

I opened one eye. Ugh. It felt really early. Why was the viserator on so loud? I heard dishes clanking downstairs and more of the news story as I closed my eye and wished my bed would swallow me up.

"With nearly fifty people departing Earth today, the *Sojourner* Mars Expedition is substantially smaller than the first endeavor. But officials assure us this is less a precautionary decision than an efficiency-based one. According to sources at the Project, this small group can quickly set up a colony and easily prepare for the arrival of a larger group."

I sat up in bed. I still had on my clothes from yesterday.

Yesterday.

If my memory was functioning, and if my brain was processing the obnoxiously loud viserator correctly, then yesterday *had* been real. We were moving to Mars. And we were leaving in—I looked at my *MonsterMetalMachines* alarm clock—eight hours.

My bedroom door burst open and Mom stood in the doorway. "Morning, sleepyhead. Today's the big d—" Her smile faded. "Michael? You slept in your clothes?"

"I guess," I muttered.

"Are you okay, Mr. Man?"

Incredi-freakin'-bull. How could she stand there like it was my birthday? I spat out a bitter laugh and looked at her coldly. "Excuse me if I'm not skipping down the hall at the thought of moving to a different *planet*, Mom." I stomped over to my closet to find something clean to wear. "One minute I'm freaked out 'cause I have a report due, and the next minute I'm freaked out because my family is going to live in *space*? Jeez, Mom. Of *course* I slept in my clothes! I barely slept at all." I tried to walk past her, but she grabbed my arm. Not hard, but tightly.

21

"Michael," she said gently, but firmly, "we've been over this." She continued in an exasperated voice. "Your father and I are on the backup team. If, for some reason, a member of first team isn't able to go on the trip, the backup members go. That's just how it is. We're trained. We're ready. And we're going."

I looked at her angrily. I was like a sofa or a viserator, being packaged up and thrown into a moving truck. Or whatever . . . moving shuttle. I wanted her to let go of my arm. If I didn't get to the shower soon, I might start crying, and I wasn't going to let her see that.

"Let go of my arm," I said to the floor, clenching my jaw. "Please."

She released me and I stormed off to the shower.

"Fast, Michael," she said. "We're leaving the house in forty-five minutes."

I took a fast shower, not because Mom told me to, but because I still had to pack. *Ha,* I thought miserably. *Pack.* We each got one box for personal possessions and the lid had to fit tight. One measly box.

I was toweling off when I heard Dad talking in a low voice out in the hallway.

"It's happening, Aurora," he said. "I have to go." There was a pause. "You should have voiced your complaints with the board—" He paused, listening to whatever Aurora was saying, then replied shortly, "I *said* it's *fine.*" He paused again. "Marie and I—" Pause. "There were never any charges to be cleared, Aurora. You of all people should know that . . ." His voice trailed off as he walked to the other end of the hallway.

Aurora is the president of the Project and works really closely with Mom and Dad. Her father, David Hazelwood, had been in charge, but he retired and dropped out of sight after the *Spirit* disaster. Dad never seemed too keen about Aurora, but I'd never heard him sound this angry on the phone before. Especially since he was talking to his boss.

There was a knock on the bathroom door and I jumped, dropping my towel into the wet tub. Great. Why didn't our house have built-in body dryers like Stinky's?

"Mike?"

"Uh, yeah?"

"Almost done? We're on a tight deadline."

"I *know,* Dad."

I heard him pound back down the stairs.

I sighed and pulled on my clothes.

I brushed some polymer into my hair to spike it up a little, bared my teeth in the mirror to make sure I had finally freed the gunk, and left the bathroom. Nita was waiting outside the door patiently . . . with a smile.

"All clean, baby brother?" she asked.

I stared at her. That was the nicest tone of voice she'd used with me in about a thousand months. She hummed a little tune and shut the bathroom door. What was going *on* in this house?

I went back into my room and tossed things into my moving box: a couple of MonsterMetalMachines that were small, my toothbrush, my readers with a few comics cards, my baseball glove. I picked up a digiframe of last year's Little League championship game. It showed me hitting a pop fly and Stinky cheering behind me. I threw it into the box and sat on my bed. *I need to talk to Stink.*

I unplugged my peapod's cord from the charging socket on my waistband. I rolled the peapod around the palm of my hand and took a deep breath. It felt like I was trying to choke down a hockey puck, but really, I guess I was just swallowing my pride.

I pressed the On button and held down the transmit pad. "Stink? You there?" I let go of the transmit pad and waited.

"Stink? Hello?"

I was about to give up when I heard a muffled "What?"

"Hey!" I felt happy for the first time in practically twenty-four hours. "Hey! You're there!"

"I'm sleeping, brain drain."

"Something crazy is going on. I need to talk to you."

"Now? Just tell me at school. I still have thirty minutes till my alarm goes off."

"No, Stinky, now. I'm not going to be at school today."

"Is this because of your report, Mike? Dude. Calm your obsessive self down."

"Just meet me at the place in like five minutes, okay?"

"You're not going to try to beat me up, are you?" He laughed, because he knew that even if I still felt mad at him, I'd never do anything like that.

"Yeah, right," I said, glad that he was laughing. "Just meet me there, okay?"

"Fine."

I left my room and walked briskly down the stairs. Instead of following the noise into the kitchen, I decided to escape out the back door. My hand was on the doorknob when I heard, "Where in the world are you going?"

"I just need to go say bye to Stinky, Dad," I said, stepping out onto the back porch.

"Oh no you're not. We're on an extraordinarily tight deadline, Mike. We don't have time for—"

"Let him go, Albert." Mom's voice filtered down the hallway. "Yeager is his best friend." I heard her start walking toward us.

"He'll be able to contact Yeager when we get to Mars," Dad argued. His scientific personality just didn't comprehend things like, well, *friends*.

"That's gonna be *months*, Dad!" I shouted.

Mom held up her hand to quiet our bickering. "He'll be back in ten minutes. Right, Mike?" I gave Mom a grateful look and bolted through the backyard.

Stinky and I got there at the same time. Our secret meeting place was a small burrow hollowed out of the side of a hill behind our neighborhood. It was close but hidden, like an easy-access private clubhouse.

Stinky looked rumply in his baggy jeans and "Elvis Is Alive" T-shirt. I told him to sit down and then I just let the whole story spill out of me.

He blinked five times in a row and said, "Are you kidding me?"

"Do I look like I'm kidding you?" I held up my hands so that he could see they were shaking. I didn't know if it was from fear or excitement, but they were jittering a mile a minute.

"Man, that is heavy news." He picked at an old candy wrapper on the ground. "You're leaving today?"

"Yeah," I said, breathless. "At two p.m."

We sat silently for a few minutes; then I looked at my watch. "I have to go, man. If I'm not back soon, my dad's going to vaporize me."

"Well," Stinky said, standing up and fidgeting with his pants, "at least you don't have to worry about your speech anymore."

"Ha." I kicked a rock over and watched two little bugs scurry out from under it. "I might not have to write it, but now I have to live it."

"Shoulda picked a project on creating your own teacher-eating Preditator."

"No doubt."

We stood there for a few seconds, not knowing what else to say.

"Well, hey," I said finally, "at least we still have these." I held up my small green peapod.

"Will that work in space?"

"It's supposed to," I said, then deepened my voice like the commercial. "This amazing device works up to one million miles away."

He looked skeptical.

"The moon is only 239,000 miles away, right? And we'll be there for at least a few weeks. Then we fly back a little closer to Earth so that we can launch from Lagrange point L1. We'll be there another week or so, I guess, and that's, what, only 200,000 miles away?"

"Dude, how do you know all this stuff?"

"I don't *always* watch *MonsterMetalMachines* on the vis. And, you know, I can read, too." I slugged him in the arm. "Anyway. These things should work until I actually take off for Mars. And the mission's gonna be in preparation mode for four weeks. I mean, I guess it is. The last mission took four weeks to . . ." I trailed off. I didn't really want to get into the whole hundreds-of-people-lost-in-space-who-are-probably-dead thing.

Stinky shifted his weight from one foot to the other. "So that's four weeks we can talk until you take off on the . . . long trip."

"You make it sound like I'm going to die or something. 'The long trip.' "

Stinky just looked at me.

I rolled my peapod between my fingers. "We'll keep in touch, okay, Stink?"

"Cool," he said, looking at the ground.

We stood awkwardly until Stinky one-arm hugged me and trotted off. I hightailed it back to the house.

I ran in through the back door and flew up the stairs to finish packing. I hadn't been in my room ten seconds when Mom burst in.

"You better get downstairs and eat breakfast, Michael. We have a long day ahead of us."

I took one last look around my room. It wasn't a huge room, or even spectacular in any way, but I'd miss it. I sighed and jammed my hands into my pockets. My fingers brushed the peapod and some grasshrinkers I must've left in there the other day. *That's one chore I won't have to do on Mars,* I thought. But that didn't make me feel better. *How can you live in a place with no grass?*

My breath caught funny in my throat.

"C'mon, Mike," Mom said softly. "Let's go eat."

Nita sat gobbling up pancakes at the kitchen table downstairs. I set my box by the front door, next to two other boxes, and then nearly had a heart attack when a humongous man in what looked like a deep red waiter's jacket tapped me on the shoulder.

"Better start eating, son. We're leaving in ten minutes."

I looked the stranger up and down. There was a gold name tag shimmering on his breast pocket. " 'Mr. Shug-ah-bert'?" I read out loud.

"The 't' is silent," he said with a big smile.

"Mr., uh, Shuga Bear? Your name is Sugar Bear?"

"It's pronounced 'Shoo-*gah*-bear,' actually. I'm your mom's executive assistant."

"My mom's who?"

"My assistant," said Mom cheerily, putting her arm around me. "You've heard me talk about Leslie before, honey. He's going to be accompanying us on our trip. He'll be making sure our every need is taken care of."

"THIS is Leslie?" I asked, shocked. "I always thought Leslie was, you know, not a dude."

Mom maneuvered me over to the table and dropped a stack of steaming pancakes in front of me. "Eat up, so we can go."

"Where's your box, cheese face?" I asked Nita as I reached for the syrup.

"I don't need a box," she answered with a smug smile. She pulled the syrup just out of my reach.

"Why not? You starting over from scratch on Mars?" I leaned over the table and snatched the syrup from her hand.

"I'm not going to Mars."

"Ha. Yeah, right." I squirted syrup onto my pancakes and shoveled in a gloopy bite.

"Seriously. I'm not going. I'm gonna live with Gram instead."

I sighed, spraying chewed-up pancake back onto my plate. I didn't know if she made up stories for attention, or what, but Nita was almost nineteen. That was way too old to be a big fat liar.

"Mom," I said, "could you please tell Nita to quit being such a pants-on-fire liar, and to go pack her box?"

Mom briefly looked uncomfortable. Then she squatted down and put on her big ol' smiley smile. Yuh-oh.

"Well, the thing is, Michael . . . ," she started, and it felt like the pancake I had just swallowed was really a ton of firecrackers.

"Nita isn't going with us."

I was dumbfounded. I could only open and shut my mouth like a floundering fish.

"She, uh . . . she didn't pass the security clearance."

Finally I spat out, *"What?!"*

Nita grinned at me from across the table and started humming a cheerful little tune that made me want to smash my pancakes in her face.

"Because of her association with *those people*, Nita wasn't approved to come on the trip. She's going to Gram's after she drops us off at the Project," Mom explained.

Mom was talking about Nita's membership in Earthlings for Earth. It's this group of people dedicated to cleaning up the environment and putting an end to off-world colonization. The EFEs don't believe that it's right for people on Earth to pollute our planet and then go do the same thing on other planets. They aren't a very radical group, mostly just a lot of noisy people with colorful hair who chain themselves to rockets. So it wasn't like Nita was some criminal mastermind. She was just my dumb sister who had dropped out of the Project Academy and was going through this dumb phase where she thought she could save the world with a bunch of other dumb people.

"Well," I huffed, standing up so quickly my chair fell over behind me. "If Nita's not going, I'm not going. I want to live with Gram, too."

Just then Dad marched into the room. "All right, everyone, it's time to go." He handed me the book from

Mrs. H. "Thanks for letting me look at this, Mike. Better put it in your box. You don't want to forget it!"

"But—" I said, not knowing what to complain about first. I didn't need that stupid book on Mars.

"Oh, here, I'll do it," he said, and grabbed the book back. He shoved it into my box.

Mom whisked my plate off the table as if the preceding five minutes had never occurred. She took Nita's plate and tossed it into the washer, too.

"Leslie, would you mind grabbing the boxes? Kids, follow me. . . ." And she headed out the front door without so much as a glance behind her.

Nita and I looked at each other—she was smiling; I was breathing fire—and then Dad shoved us along. The drivedropper spat out the electri-car and the doors slid open.

I stammered, "But, I don't want— I'm not go—"

"Oh, everything is going to be fine, honey," Mom said, patting my arm as she gently pushed me into my seat. "Don't you worry about a thing. Belt."

A chorus of "belt"s filled the e.c. My mind raced and my heart careened around my chest. Why didn't Nita pack any of her stuff to bring to Gram's? Come to think of it, what was going to happen to all our stuff back home while we were gone? What about my simulator games and the vis recorder? How was I going to record all the *MonsterMetalMachines* episodes? There were so many questions; it was all happening too fast. I mean, if I'd had more time to think about it, I might have been possibly, sort of, maybe *excited* about becoming a space traveler. But right now it was like everything was spinning away from me. There wasn't time to grapple with what was happening. I felt lost and we were still in the driveway.

Mr. Shugabert leaned around from the passenger's seat and said, "Everyone comfortable?" He didn't wait for a response. "Excellent." He flashed a beaming smile of what looked like hundreds of teeth. "I am so *stoked*."

The e.c. whirred to life. I took one last look at our house, at the light blue shutters I'd helped Dad paint last summer, at the unshrunken grass. And then we were off.

It didn't take very long to drive to the Project. That was why Mom and Dad had bought our house in the first place. It was close to their work and they could get there quickly in case of an emergency. Mom's a mission coordinator and Dad's a mission doctor. And when bad things started happening with the first Mars mission, it was lucky they lived so close. They practically took sleeping bags to the office. Those times really stunk.

My mind snapped back in gear as the electri-car slowed. All our seat belts popped off at the same time. The doors slid open and we stepped out in front of the Project. Mr. Shugabert got our boxes from the trunk. Mom and Dad and Nita hugged and Mom said they'd be checking in on her during the once-a-week Earthbound communication each family was allowed. It was like Nita was going to summer camp. I just glared at her, not really thinking about the fact that it would literally take engineering feats of spaceflight to see her again.

Finally she grabbed me, gave me a big hug, and whispered in my ear, "Watch out for anything strange." She kissed the top of my head and said in a low voice, "Help me try to find Hubble."

Then she got back into the electri-car. What was she talking about? How could we find Hubble? We'd already tried. He was gone, along with everyone else who had been on the *Spirit*.

Nita sped off.

Mom and Dad walked to the front doors of the Project with their heads high and smiles on their faces. It was like they abandoned their firstborn child every day. Mr. Shugabert led the way, carrying our boxes. The Project's doors slid open as he scanned his ID badge. I watched Mom and Dad walk into the building and I felt sick to my stomach.

Inside, it was killer. I momentarily forgot my sick feeling as I felt a glimmer of excitement bubble up from my toes. The control room blinked and glittered like a supernova. People ran around with handhelds and shouted into their collartalks. Huge holoboards hung on the far wall. One holoboard showed the shuttle preparing for liftoff.

Another showed SpacePort and the *Sojourner* spacecraft orbiting around the moon.

The last one had a grainy picture on it. It looked like just a blank black screen until you really stared at it. In the middle floated a seething mass. It looked kind of like the vapors you see rising from the road on a hot day. The Fold. Every now and then a shimmer of color shot around the Fold's edges. As scary as it seemed, it looked awesome. That was our shortcut to Mars, and I still couldn't believe our ship was going into that thing. It looked like it was just waiting to eat us and then give a yellow burp.

Then the Fold disappeared and was replaced by something huge and pink. What was it?

The picture focused.

A tongue!

The image widened and some teeth closed into a grotesque smile. The brightest blue braces I'd ever seen took up the whole screen. The camera pulled back farther, revealing the grinning face of the palest girl this side of the moon. She turned her face side to side and I could see that she was talking nonstop, but there was no sound. A few minutes later she was gone and the lurching Fold was back up on the screen.

Mr. Shugabert disappeared into an elevator with our boxes, but not without giving me an idiotic grin first. This guy . . . it was like he lived his whole life in a chewing gum commercial or something.

Mom tugged my arm and led me and Dad to the other side of the room. As we walked, they greeted some vaguely familiar people with a wave. A tall man with round glasses waved back. I might have seen him at last year's Project employee picnic. Seemed like we had talked about robots while we'd waited for the bathroom. I followed Mom and Dad to the elevator where he stood.

"Jim," Dad said in his professional voice. He nodded in the man's direction.

"Albert, Marie," Jim said back, nodding at them.

"This is our son, Michael," Dad said as if I was an alien or a ham steak for sale.

"I think we met at the picnic last year," Jim said, smiling. I smiled back, but my grin faded when the pale girl from the holoboard bounded up next to us.

"Albert, Marie . . . Michael . . . this is my daughter, Larc."

"Hello, ma'am, sir, child of ma'am and sir," the gangly girl said, flashing us a glimpse of those crazy blue braces.

In the elevator, I tried to get a good look at Larc. Tall like her dad, pointy bird nose, practically clear blue eyes. I looked away as she caught my eye and smiled.

The elevator jolted up a few stories and we popped out in an empty, stark white hallway. Everyone piled out of the elevator. Mom gave my shoulders a squeeze and said, "Don't look so freaked out. We're just going to the locker rooms to get changed. Oh, and, Mike? Make sure to leave your clothes—and everything in your pockets—in the locker you're provided. No outside communication devices are allowed on the ship."

How did she know I had my peapod?! I hope when I'm a parent, I can be psychic, too. I made a face and walked into the locker room.

A few minutes later, back in the elevator, Mom and Dad exchanged looks. I chewed my lip. I felt like an idiot dressed in a shiny kite. These jumpsuits were ridiculous. And why did Mom and Dad keep looking at each other like that? They kept glancing at each other like they were trying to communicate telepathically.

I rolled the peapod around in my pocket, along with the grasshrinkers I'd brought with me, breaking the rules. I wanted to keep my ties to Earth, I guess. Besides, I'd only been away from home for like an hour and I already had a million things to tell Stinky.

We all rode the elevator up to the fifth floor. I'd been there a million times. Mom and Dad have their offices on the fifth floor. I felt a small wave of comfort settle in as I stepped onto familiar ground. There were a whole bunch of people in there, too, even some kids. Most of them looked just like I felt. Totally freaked out. That was a little comforting, too.

Mom tapped me on the shoulder and I jumped about three feet.

"Can you sit on that bench outside my office, honey? Dad and I will be right back."

I did what she said, fighting my impulse to argue.

*Be calm. Brave. Make them feel guilty,* I decided as I sat down. *Nerves of steel. Nerves of steel.* They hurried toward a cluster of adults standing by a large computer screen.

"Mars, huh?"

I jumped again. So much for nerves of steel. I whipped my head around. Larc had snuck up behind me and sat on the bench. She was staring at me with her icy blue eyes.

I hung my head in my hands. "I guess."

"Aren't you excited?" she asked. "It's a new world. And we're the pioneers."

I looked at her like she was insane.

"What kind of a name is Larc, anyway?" I asked. That was rude of me, but I was too freaked to care.

"It's Carl spelled backwards," she said.

I thought for a second. "No, it isn't. Carl spelled backwards is L-R-A-C."

She shrugged like I was wrong and she was right.

I closed my eyes and tried to pretend she wasn't there. My brain was on the verge of going, "Okay. Whatever. Initiate shutdown. I'm just going to hum the theme song to *MonsterMetalMachines* now." I wondered if this was how Nita felt most of the time. That made me laugh and I thought about what she had said. Something about finding Hubble and watching out? Even talking about finding Hubble was crazy.

"What's so funny?" Larc asked, leaning in my face. Her white hair brushed my shoulder with a swish.

I started to slide away but Dad suddenly reappeared. I jumped up. "Okay, Michael," he said with a serious look. "We're all set. Let's go take our seats on the shuttle." He gave me a short, squeezy hug that seemed totally out of place and weird. "I know this is an exciting day for you. It's exciting for all of us."

I shook my head. If he'd paid attention to me for two seconds that morning, he'd have seen that I was anything *but* excited about this trip. Well, except that I did feel kind of excited. We *were* going into space, after all. I've been learning about space since practically before I was born. My nursery had little rocket ships on the wall. So the idea of really, truly going into space; really, truly stepping on a different planet . . . Well, deep down inside I *was* excited. But I would never let Mom and Dad know that.

Outside on the launchpad, the shuttle was hulking, smoking, and vibrating. Its sheer giganticness blocked out the sun—like a giant blue beehive. It couldn't be a good sign that my first impression of the ship was that it reminded me of Mrs. Halebopp. Not a good sign at all.

41

**We are all** *going to die.*

I gripped the bar in front of me. It shook fiercely, like the bolts might come loose at any moment. I tried to look at Dad, but the g-forces were so strong I couldn't move my head even a millimeter. It felt like the world's strongest vacuum cleaner was sucking my cheeks out through the back of my head.

My teeth were dried out and my tongue felt like it was coated in sand. Not the time to hyperventilate.

Really. Not.

The. Time.

The last time I'd hyperventilated, it had been at the doctor's office, so that had worked out pretty well. But there weren't any nurses here with paper bags. Only fantastically loud roaring, violent shaking, and invisible headrest vacuums.

And fire. Did I mention fire? Because nobody told me there was going to be fire. Out of the corner of my bulging eye, I saw yellow and orange flashes. They cast my whole row into jumping shadows.

*We are going to die,* I thought again, refusing to scream like the other children. *Nerves of steel. Nerves of steel.* I wanted to meet my fate like a man. Even if just a hyperventilating man in a shiny jumpsuit.

Up the aisle, I caught a glimpse of the cockpit, where Mom sat. As mission coordinator, she communicated with Mission Control and made sure the ship stayed on course. I saw darts of her black hair shaking in the hurly-burly of early takeoff.

As we rocketed out of Earth's atmosphere, the shuttle slowed down and eventually leveled off. We floated for a few minutes, tethered to our seats by our seat belts, and then we were sucked back into our seats. I got this queasy, gutter-ball feeling in my stomach. The captain had turned on the AutoGrav. The children calmed down now (though I could hear one blowing chunks from the AutoGrav) and Mom made an announcement letting us all know that the turbulence was over.

With the g-forces a rapidly fading nightmare now, I

turned to Dad and growled, "You didn't tell me about the shooting flames."

He shook his head and said, "Mike. How many takeoffs have you watched from the back porch? A thousand?"

I shrugged, and despite myself, my grimace turned into an embarrassed grin. He was right. And in every single one of them, I never actually saw the shuttle; it was more like a ball of flame reaching into the sky.

"I'll be right back," Dad said abruptly. He manually unclicked his seat belt and lumbered toward the cockpit. He stopped about three rows behind the cockpit and bent down to talk to Jim. Dad pulled his medical kit out of his jumpsuit and offered Jim a small vial. Jim took the vial and shook Dad's hand. Larc turned around in her seat and waved at me. In the semidarkness of the cabin, her stark white hair looked almost lit up from inside.

Dad was coming back to our row when a hand shot out from a seat and grabbed his wrist. It was Mr. Shugabert.

Dad leaned down toward him and said something like "medical necessity," and then the hand let go of his wrist.

"What was that all about?" I asked when he jolted back down the aisle.

"I just gave Larc's father a vitamin serum for her. She's a little sick from the ride and this is a new serum specially formulated to settle a queasy stomach."

"No," I said, shaking my head. "With him." I pointed. "Why is Sugar Bear so grabby?"

"Oh." Dad shrugged. "He was just saying hi."

"Why is he even here, anyway?"

"It's no big deal, Mike. Your mom is a busy lady and busy people need assistants. Plain and simple. The Project thought it would be nice for Mr. Shugabert to come along and help take care of things for the family. That way Mom and I can more easily concentrate on the mission."

"A babysitter," I said grimly.

"Don't be silly. He's an *executive assistant*."

I gave Dad a dubious look.

"You'll hardly even notice he's on the trip."

"Right," I said, watching Dad scratch his nose. Hubble once taught Stinky and me that if someone's scratching his nose while talking it is the number one sign that that person is lying.

Hubble.

"So, what about Nita?" I asked. I wondered if I should mention to Dad that Nita had asked me to look for Hubble. Ever since the first mission—when everything went wrong and Hubble was lost—well, she hardly ever mentioned his name anymore. It was so weird that she'd mentioned him this morning. I rubbed my temples. The thought of Nita not coming on the trip still made my stomach churn. Or maybe that was the AutoGrav.

"She should be at Gram's by now. I'll see what I can find out when we get on the ship. You know we're not allowed any personal Earth-bound messages, right?" He looked at me skeptically. "No peapods. No handheld IMs. It futzes with the systems."

"I *know*, Dad," I said irritably. "One Earth-bound call, per family, per week," I chirped, imitating Mom. I slouched in my seat, grumbling. Why did everyone always think I wasn't paying attention when they talked?

The shuttle slowed to a stop with a loud click. Everyone looked around nervously. Then Mom came through the cockpit doors.

"Everyone," she said, with her eyes dancing and a smile threatening to engulf her whole face, "we've just established air lock. We're connected to the *Sojourner* now and we should be opening the door any minute."

There was a pause and then a smattering of half-hearted claps that turned into a roar of applause. I guess I wasn't the only one who thought we were gonna die. I joined in the clapping. It stunk smelly gerbils to be moving, but it would have stunk a lot more to blow up on the shuttle flight!

Mom walked over to me and Dad and squeezed our shoulders.

"We've made it," she said. She sounded almost relieved.

Dad kissed her cheek and then stuffed something

into Mom's flight suit pocket. It looked like another vial of that vitamin stuff.

Mom started off toward the cockpit and patted the pocket Dad had just "secretly" invaded. "I'll see you on board," she said to us over her shoulder.

Our seat belts automatically unclicked, and the other passengers gathered up their readers and carry-on bags. You could tell that everyone was a little apprehensive and nervous . . . even most of the grown-ups. But it had been a rather exciting hour.

Dad handed me a clear vial of vitamin stuff. "Here's to keeping the queasies away," he said, offering up his own vial to toast. I glowered. He was always making me and Nita gobble down vitamins, minerals, and frankenfoods. Every time Dad gave me something to put in my mouth, it made me want to puke. I held the vial up and examined it. The liquid was clear, but gross specks floated around. Silvery chunks, even. Blech.

He clinked his vial with mine, even though I didn't hold it up for the toast. "Bottoms up, kiddo," he said. I pinched my nose and chugged. Shockingly, it didn't taste that bad. Kind of minty.

We made our way down the aisle and walked through the air lock.

Then . . . wow.

The *Sojourner*'s lobby was four or five stories high, and very long and skinny, like Fierce Mangle (the best

MonsterMetalMachine ever). Gray railings on each level formed long rings around the inside of the ship. On each floor, white doors stood out from the dark walls. They had no windows or doorknobs or anything.

Straight ahead, far down at the end of the tube-shaped ship, was a huge window that bubbled out into space. That end of the ship must have been three and a half football fields away.

There was a sign on a table just inside the air lock. It said "Welcome to the *Sojourner*! Please take your mapper!" The mappers were stacked and labeled alphabetically.

I ran up and grabbed the mapper labeled "Stellar." It was a tiny little box. I pressed a red button in the center and a hologram of the ship hovered over the box.

"Cool," I said quietly.

"Cool what?"

I jumped. Mom had snuck up behind me.

I held up the mapper for her. "Yep. Pretty cool," she said.

"Come on, let's get going, you two," Dad said. He acted impatient, but I could tell he liked the mapper, too.

The hologram showed a hovering arrow over a doorway in the back of the projected little ship. The arrow was labeled "Stellar Residence."

I pointed and said, "Home sweet home." We started walking to our new apartment. We passed the cafeteria and the public bathrooms and even what looked like the captain's quarters. We kept walking and walking, down one hallway and up another . . . around one corner and through a doorway . . . Finally it seemed like we were getting close. I noticed the only people still hunting around were us and Jim and Larc.

Jim was chatting with Dad about simulated nerve impulses or something boring like that when I caught a glimpse of a figure behind our little group.

Mr. Shugabert was tailing us.

I tugged on Mom's flight suit and jerked my head in Mr. Shugabert's direction.

"Why's Sugar Bear lurking back there?" I asked.

"Oh, Mike," Mom said, laughing. "He's not lurking; he's following us." She turned around and waved at him. "His apartment should be right next to ours. Adjoining, probably."

My eyes widened. Chewing Gum Commercial Dude was going to be practically living with us? Bleh. Who needs extra grown-ups around, anyway?

When we went up to our doorway, the mapper beeped and a little drawer opened from the side. Inside was a flash key.

"For emergency use only" was written across both sides of the flash key. Dad grabbed my hand.

"Hey. Don't use that. Look: the apartments are equipped with a retinal scanner."

He pressed his right eye into a small indentation on the door frame. We heard a buzz and a ding, and the door whooshed open.

We waved to Larc and Jim; then Dad swept around and grabbed Mom. He picked her up with her legs hanging over his arm, her arm around his neck, and her butt sagging in the middle. I covered my eyes with my hands.

She hooted. Dad said very solemnly, "I must carry my bride over the threshold of a new home."

He marched inside with Mom kicking her legs happily. I wanted to make a smart-mouth comment, but it felt weird without Nita. I actually missed her.

Dad set Mom down and smiled at me. "Well, get in here, Mike."

I walked through the doorway and into the apartment. I glanced over my shoulder just as the door was shutting behind me, and I saw Mr. Shugabert walking into the apartment next to ours. He caught my eye and this time he wasn't smiling.

The door closed and I felt a chill. The exact kind of chill you're not supposed to feel on a seventy-two-degree climate-controlled ship.

I have to say, I was not impressed. This apartment was teeny-weeny. Wait. Not teeny-weeny. Teeeeeeeeeeny. Weeeeeeeeeeny. Especially compared with the size of the ship. If every apartment on the ship was this size, they could stuff the entire population of Star City in here. As it was, there were only about fifty people on this mission—with maybe ten kids added to that. It seemed crazy for the ship to be so huge, with so many tiny apartments. What did the Project think, we were going to go to Mars and find a colony of aliens to ship home? Heck, even then we could all have our *own* apartments. Actually, that would be spankin' awesome.

I walked over to a wall and pushed a small square button. A table floated down from the ceiling and two benches slid out from under it. They were the color of scorched metal. And I would know. Stinky and I once tried to smelt some old MonsterMetalMachines with Hubble's plasma laser. It didn't work.

Dad patted the tabletop and I pushed the button again. The benches slid back and the whole thing floated back up. It was crazy cool.

With a goofy I'm-a-dork-and-I-love-gadgets grin, I pushed another button and a small viserator popped out of the wall. My mouth fell open. I had never seen such a little viserator. This thing was the definition of "teeny-weeny" (emphasis on "weeny"). I started to complain about the obvious futility of such a small vis, but Mom held up her hand.

"I don't want to hear it," she said. "You're lucky we have one at all. Not everyone does. And you watch too much vis as it is. Now you'll have more time to concentrate on school."

Great.

Dad hollered, "Hey, Mike, come look at this!" He was in front of an enormous window. It took up the entire back wall of the room. We could see white stars and red stars and blue stars and even a little bit of Earth up in the corner. Dad flipped a switch and the lights went out. This made everything outside the window seem even brighter and more sparkly.

"Spectacular," he breathed.

Mom walked up to the window and put her hand on

it. I did the same thing and for a moment all three of us were quiet, just staring out at the stars and the Earth and the black void around us.

"Well, Marie . . . ," Dad said a few minutes later as he randomly pressed on a wall, looking for more buttons. "I'm flummoxed. Where are the bedrooms and bathrooms?"

Mom smiled. She walked over to the super-giant window and pushed a small button on the sill—a button I had missed in my button-pushing parade.

Now, really, this was the coolest thing so far. The window slid out into space! As it slid, windows appeared on both sides of it so that it was a kind of three-walled window—like a pop-out wall on those antique campers in the Star City RV Museum.

Then those side windows started to slide out to the right and the left as the big window stretched along with them, making a long, clear tube. Finally a new wall popped out of the floor on each side of us. This whole new section of window-rooms expanded our apartment so that it looked like these rooms were a very big blob of dew hanging on to the side of the ship.

Mom motioned at the new space. "This," she said, "is where our rooms are."

We stepped over the sill into the new space. The whole thing was clear, so when I looked down, I could see stars and deep black space. It made my stomach jump. This window-room was a kind of foyer. To the right was a doorway. This was Mom and Dad's room. Once through the doorway, Dad moved around the room, pushing little clear buttons on the walls. Bedroom furniture appeared. When the bed rolled out, there was an old-fashioned book lying on the mattress.

"Hey, look at this, Marie!" Dad picked the book up. "A gift from the captain." He ran his hand over the pages. I tried to see but he clapped it shut and stuck it on a bookshelf attached to the bed's headboard.

Dad pushed another button. In a corner, a nozzle stuck out of the wall. It looked like a showerhead. "You can't just take a shower in the corner of the room," I said, confused.

Mom came over. "Push the button next to the nozzle, Mike."

I pushed it and two more walls whooshed up beside me, enclosing me in a triangle of clear plastic. The walls mottled themselves so that no one could see in. A seat appeared and I thought, *Oh, boy, I hope that's a toilet*. I lifted the lid. Yep. A toilet. A weird one, made of plastic and with no water, but a toilet just the same.

"Hey, Dad," I said, "I found the bathroom."

I heard mumbling between Mom and Dad but I couldn't make out exact words. I pushed the button on top of the toilet and it disappeared into the wall. I really hope it flushed. Then the bathroom walls slid down into the floor. Mom and Dad were huddled in the far corner of the room, whispering.

"I don't know why you gave it to him," Mom said, sounding a little distressed.

"It was just precautionary," said Dad.

"It's dangerous, that's what it is," she snapped. But right then she saw me.

"Hey, you!" She smiled a bit crazily. "What'd you think of the bathroom?"

I stared at them for a minute and said, "Um, it's pretty cool. I've never whizzed in a toilet like that before."

Mom's smile faded in a flash and she rolled her eyes. She's not a fan of the word "whizzed" when it refers to peeing. (She likes "whizzed" to describe something you'd do to a test. Like "Hey, I got every answer right and totally whizzed that test." How dumb is that? It sounds like you peed on your test.)

Across the hall was my room. When I stepped into it, I was happy to see that the floor was mottled just like the bathroom walls had been. I was also happy to see a shower nozzle sticking out of the far corner. My own bathroom. Wow. I didn't even have my own bathroom on Earth. Nita would be jealous. (Gram only has one bathroom and it's pink and reeks of cream deodorant.)

I started pushing various buttons on the walls. Bed.

Desk. Chair. Computer thing labeled "Personal Homework Station." What the heck was *that*? A fake computer? I made a face and was on my way to investigate it further when I heard a voice.

"Hi, Mike."

I whirled around. There was no one in the room with me.

"The time is five-twenty-three. Are you ready for dinner?"

"Who's there?" I asked quietly. "Is that . . . is that you, Mr. Shugabert?"

"Dinner will be ready in approximately twenty-two minutes," the voice drawled.

"Uh, okay," I whispered, looking around. I backed slowly out of my room and ran back into the living area. Disembodied voices—especially one *in my bedroom*—generally scare the bejeebers out of me.

Mom and Dad were milling around near the viserator, talking quietly again. Mom came over and put her hand on my shoulder. "Mike? You look like you've seen a ghost."

"Nah." I shrugged. "It's only Mr. Shugabert *spying on me in my room*." I shivered. "That's all."

"Oh, Mike. He's not spying," Dad said. "Mr. Shugabert has just prepared the apartment for us. That's all."

" 'Prepared'?" I asked.

Dad sounded like he was explaining something I

should know already. "For our convenience, Mike. He's rigged the place with voice-automated systems to work as your alarm clock, study guide, channel-changer, et cetera, et cetera."

Mom chimed in. "This way Mr. Shugabert is omnipresent, Mike. Anything we need, he's here to get it for us." She nervously shuffled her feet, but then she smiled. "Cool, huh?"

I didn't care what Mom said. Having a weird, overly friendly dude always at my beck and call gave me a creepy crawly feeling. Especially when his disembodied voice was eager to help me out, too.

## Pitch-black.

Where was I? My heart thumped a million miles a minute. I sat bolt upright, whipping my head around. As the sleep drained from my brain, I remembered that I was in my room on the *Sojourner*. I gave my nose a quick tug and wondered why my eyes weren't adjusting. I couldn't see *any*thing.

"You rise early, Mike," said the voice of Shugabert. "Your breakfast isn't ready yet."

"What . . . ," I said, pulling the covers closer. "Why are you in my room, Sugar Bear?"

"You rise early, Mike," the voice of Shugabert said again. "Your breakfast isn't ready yet."

It was a recording.

"Mr. Shugabert?" I asked again, tentatively.

"It is approximately four-thirty-one in the morning. Mr. Shoo-*gah*-bear is still sleeping. Should you need him, please knock gently on the adjoining door."

"Lights," I said.

A soft glow filled the room and I could see the windows and my partially unpacked box.

"Mr. Shoo-*gah*-bear is still sleeping," the recording repeated.

"Off," I commanded. "Stop. End program."

"I do not understand your request," the creepy voice said. "This voice-automated system only serves as a complimentary notification servi—"

"Go away, vamoose, get out of here! Turn off!" This voice was creeping me out.

"Please rephrase your request."

"*Leave!*" I shouted.

"Leaves are green, flattened, lateral structures attached to stems and functioning as principal organs of photosynthesis and transpiration in most plants."

"Wha— No, not 'leaf,' you moron. *Leave. L-e-a-v-e.*"

"For your convenience, please knock on the adjoining door. Mr. Shoo-*gah*-bear will be with you as soon as he's available."

"Great," I muttered, hopping out of bed and searching my box for my favorite *MonsterMetalMachines* towel. "I'm living in a perpetual voice mail system."

While I showered, I had a brain wave that I should

go out and explore the ship a bit. So after my shower, I pulled on my jumpsuit and shoes. I snuck out of the apartment and headed for the lobby.

After rounding a corner, I jogged down the stairs— and felt a hand on my shoulder. I turned. Mr. Shugabert was standing there, his red jacket spotless, a little doodad in his ear almost completely hidden. He looked refreshed, as if he always stood around on stairways at four-thirty in the morning.

"Where are you off to so early?" he asked cheerfully, though it seemed like his eyes narrowed a bit when he looked at me.

"Just out for a jog," I said, feeling my face flush. I hated that. I wasn't even doing anything wrong. Well, except for the sneaking-out-of-the-apartment-at-four-thirty part.

"A jog?" He raised his eyebrows.

I shrugged. "Sure."

"Do your parents know where you are?" His voice sounded as if he was talking to a three-year-old who was just caught eating cookies before dinner.

I didn't say anything. He leaned over so that we were face to face.

He smiled another one of those chewing-gum-commercial smiles. "You really shouldn't be out here like this, Mike. Spaceships can be dangerous for little boys. You don't want to get hurt, do you?" I could smell his hot breath. It did not smell like fresh mint. And I did not appreciate being called a little boy.

"I'll be fine," I finally managed to sputter.

Shugabert stood up and placed both hands on my shoulders. With more pressure than he really needed, he twisted me around until I was facing the opposite direction. "Go back to your apartment, Mike, and I'll pretend like this never happened."

"I told you, Sugar Bear," I said, starting to get mad, "I'm just out for a . . . a jog. I couldn't sleep."

Another red-jacketed guy I'd never seen before came up to us. He frowned at me and whispered something into Mr. Shugabert's ear. I felt Mr. Shugabert's hands release my shoulders.

"I have to go take care of something, Mike," Mr. Shugabert said. "I'll see you back at your apartment." He nodded slowly, as if the movement of his head would make me nod, too. He started to walk away but stopped and turned around. "I'd hate for your parents to find out about you sneaking out. That'd be a shame, wouldn't it? Getting punished on your first day as a space traveler?" He was smiling the whole time he talked, but he somehow didn't look all that happy. There was something more than just condescending about that guy. Then he was up the stairs and out of sight.

My heart beating a little faster than normal, I stood there, thinking about going back to the apartment and getting into bed. But something inside me started to burn, like the glow on a handheld screen just after you turn it off. I felt my cheeks warming. Who was he to tell me what to do? He wasn't my dad. He wasn't my teacher. Heck, my mom was the mission coordinator. I should be able to do anything I want.

I narrowed my eyes and continued down the stairs, directly into the lobby. I admit, I did throw a quick glance over my shoulder to make sure Mr. Shugabert was gone. But when I was positive he was nowhere in sight, I felt braver. Though as I got farther into the lobby, what I mostly felt was disappointment. It looked the same as it had when I'd first seen it. I thought there might be some fun things I'd initially missed—like a waterfall or an antigravity chamber. But there was nothing like that. Just some trees, a few bushes, and holograms of different solar systems floating over benches. Bo-oring.

I jogged in place and decided to check out the school. Best to familiarize yourself with the enemy as soon as possible. I was leaving the lobby when, out of the corner of my eye, I saw a narrow hallway jutting back behind one of the benches. I got this funny feeling in my stomach: the hallway was probably blocked off for a reason, but my curiosity got the better of me.

At home my curiosity was always getting the better of me. I'd sneak into Nita's room so that I could find all her EFE propaganda and hide it. And Stinky and I used to bust into Hubble's room and look for dirty reader cards under his mattress. Just the idea that someone was trying to hide something from me made me want to tear down walls to find it.

I followed my pounding gut. Why did I feel so nervous? I did stuff like this all the time. And yet I caught myself breathing shallowly and looking over my shoulder. It was that stupid Sugar Bear. I didn't think my parents would be thrilled with me for sneaking out if he caught me and brought me back to them.

I grabbed the bench with one hand and stuffed the other in my pocket, trying a one-handed bench-hopping maneuver popular with the *MonsterMetalMachine* skateboarding mandroid, PunkBot. Woo! I successfully hopped the bench and tried to go down the hallway, but *ooooof*. It was like I suddenly weighed forty-five thousand pounds. I couldn't lift my feet, and my arms felt like they were being stretched to the floor. It was like I was stuck in an invisible tar pit or something.

After ten minutes I hadn't even made it an inch. It must be a gravity enhancement net. Fantastic. These stupid gravity enhancers were the newest in security, at least according to a thing I saw on the vis.

I sighed hopelessly. I couldn't even yell for help; it felt like I'd need at least twenty strong dudes hefting a crowbar to get my mouth open. I struggled to move my eyes around so that I could get a better sense of my surroundings. I was only about half a foot away from the bench, so that meant anyone walking through the lobby would see me. I was so busted.

Then, on the wall, about three feet above me and two feet ahead of me, I saw a spider skitter up onto the ceiling. I had never been so happy to see a spider before in my life! Thank goodness for spaceships with "natural" atmospheres. That spider proved that the net I was caught in wasn't very big. So if I could just wiggle forward or up or . . . I noticed that there was a small grate under my left foot. It was smaller than my foot, actually, so there was no way I could escape that way, unless . . .

I used all my strength to wiggle a finger in my pocket. It barely grazed a grasshrinker. If I could pop it and get some juice on my fingertip, it might be enough to get me through the grate. Or it might be too much and disappear me completely.

I took as deep a breath as I could muster underneath all the pressure of the net and I scraped my fingernail against the skin of the grasshrinker. It didn't work. Those things have thick skins for a reason. I had nothing else to do, though, and nowhere else to go, so I stood there for what felt like forever, scritch-scratching at the grasshrinker in my pocket until I felt a little moisture on my finger. Then a gush. And then . . .

I was falling.

Falling.

Freaking out.

Falling some more. And *oof.* I landed with a tiny thump. I had fallen through the grate and was free of the gravity net. Of course, I was also now about six inches tall. Sigh.

Well, from past experience, I knew that it took a couple of hours to resize after, uh, "accidentally" shrinking oneself. So I hustled as fast as my tiny, tiny legs could carry me, searching for an escape.

After a while, I looked up and saw another grate. I climbed up some wires, pretending they were those awful ropes from gym class, and once I was at the top, I scrambled through the grate. Just in time, too, because I felt my body lurch as it began the resizing process.

I was now about two feet tall. I looked around and saw that I was back in the hallway but past the net. Yay! I made my way forward, feeling more and more curious. It felt like I was moving downhill, into the belly of the ship. Down, down, down I walked, losing all sense of where I was in the ship. *This is probably just a shortcut to the mainframe*, I thought. But, no, that couldn't be it. Because up ahead I saw a soft blue glow. And a noise like a faraway hive of bees. I felt another lurch as I resized some more. I was already almost normal size.

The hallway made a sharp right turn. The glow

seemed brighter. I held my breath as I inched toward the turn. . . . The light grew deeper, the buzzing louder.

Wait. What was—?

Oh no.

No. No. No.

*"Arrrghhhh!"*

**Someone had tapped** me on the shoulder. Hard. How had anyone gotten past that net? Expecting to see Shugabert—or a floating antigravity monster—I swallowed and hastily prepared a lame speech about how I was miserably lost and my mapper was broken and I was on my way back to my apartment, et cetera, et cetera. But when I turned around to see who it was . . .

Dad!

And he did not look happy.

"Michael," he said gruffly, "what are you doing?"

"I . . . ," I said, completely forgetting the lie. "Uh . . ."

"Let's go." He stepped behind me and poked me in the back. "March."

"But, Dad," I whined, sort of regaining my composure. "What's down there? What's that noise?"

"What's down there?" he asked, his eyes shooting sparks and narrowing into two small slits. "You want to know what's down there?"

I hesitated, not liking how red his face was.

Dad huffed, "Three weeks of no viserator is down that hallway."

"Da-ad!"

"Shhh!" He glanced around nervously and grabbed my arm. He growled in a low voice, "Never being trusted by your parents again. *That's* what's down that hallway."

"But . . . !" I said, tripping as he dragged me closer to the doorway.

"But nothing!" Dad spat. "You don't get to talk right now." He stopped and looked me straight in the eyes. "Did you even *think* about how your mom and I would feel when we woke up and you weren't there?"

He was blowing this way out of proportion. I mean, come on. This was a spaceship. It wasn't like I could get lost or hit by an electri-bus. I looked at the floor, feeling ashamed and then feeling angry at feeling ashamed.

His grip tightened on my arm as he used his other hand to punch a concealed button. The gravity enhancement net powered down with a dying buzz. We walked through the doorway and he dragged me over the bench. He pushed another button hidden right in the middle of the wall and I heard the doorway buzz back to life. He looked both ways before we set out into the lobby, like there really *was* a chance of us getting hit by an electri-bus. Then we walked briskly and silently back to the apartment.

Inside, Mom nearly suffocated me with a bone-crushing hug.

"Thank God," she sighed into my ear, and I felt her wet cheek pressed against my face. "Don't ever, *ever* do anything like that again," she said, and her vise-grip hug softened. "We *told* you not to go out on your own. What were you thinking?"

I wiggled out of her grip. "I was thinking that I'm on a spaceship and it's not like I can get lost or anything. Plus, you never said anything about me not going out! Ask the robotic, disembodied Sugar Bear. He probably has recordings of all our conversations. You never said anything." I pouted and no one spoke for a minute. Mom blew her nose. "What is the *deal* with you guys?" I asked. "I just went to check things out. That's all."

The parentals stared angrily, so I added, "I was, uh, just trying to map out a good way to get to class. You know, so that I won't be late on my first day."

"Ever heard of a mapper?" Mom asked icily, swiping at her cheeks. I stood there wondering why they were making such a big deal out of this.

Then I thought of something peculiar.

"How did you know where I was? I mean, you woke up and just knew to go look in a secret hallway at the other end of the lobby? Did Mr. Shugabert tell you where I was? And how did you know where those buttons were?"

"We haven't seen Mr. Shugabert this morning," Mom said. "And how did *you* get past the security measures?"

Ignoring her question (Mom thinks shrinking yourself is dangerous, no matter what the commercials say), I answered, "Well, *I* saw Sugar Bear and he was creepy. He was all trying to get me to go back to the apartment and threatening to snitch on me."

"He's just doing his job, Mike," Mom said, rolling her eyes. "He's not creepy; he's looking *out* for you."

After a few seconds Dad cleared his throat. "Anyway, Mr. Shugabert didn't say anything. I just woke up and you were gone. When I went to look for you, I saw that the gravity net had changed color, indicating an anomaly. When I went to check it out, I saw you ducking around a corner." He talked quickly and scratched his nose as he spoke.

Then Mom broke in. "It doesn't matter how we found you, Michael. What matters is that you are in big trouble. Big trouble. Now eat something and get to class. We'll talk about this . . . *incident* later." She gave me an and-I-mean-business look and went to her room.

Dad threw a plate of cold eggs onto the table and said stiffly, "Eat."

I had choked down about two forkfuls when he thrust another vial of the vitamin serum at me.

"Drink this, too. You'll need your energy, since you were up so early this morning."

I broke the seal on the vial and took a minty sip. It did not go well with the eggs. I was about to ask if I had to drink the whole thing when Mr. Shugabert's disembodied voice broke in and said, "Mike. School starts in approximately fifteen minutes. For optimal arrival time, you should leave in two minutes."

"See there," Dad grumbled. "You don't even need to map out a route."

I pushed my plate away and went into my room without a word. I grabbed my school stuff and marched to the front door.

"Hey," Dad said as I pushed the button and the door whooshed open. "I need you to take this with you." He shoved an old book at me. It was the one that had been on his mattress the night before.

"Why?" I asked. I didn't want to lug some heavy thing with me the whole day.

"Your teacher is an expert on these things and I'd like her to look at the binding. I'm worried it's in bad shape."

"Whatever," I said, snatching the book from him.

"Be gentle with it, Mike," he said impatiently. "Don't let any pages fall out."

"Fine!" I said. I shoved it in my bag and stomped out the door.

"What is their problem?" I muttered to myself, walking down the hall in front of our apartment. I just couldn't figure out why Mom and Dad were acting so protective and weird. And what was that blue light, anyway? And the humming noise? Maybe I could pop by on my way home from class this afternoon. After all, I now knew where those handy buttons were located. . . .

"Hello."

I wheeled around and saw Larc walking next to me, her feet perfectly in step with mine.

"Uh, hello," I said.

"Your name is Mike."

"That's right," I said, instinctively not being too friendly.

"My name is Larc."

"I know," I said, giving her a quizzical look. "We met yesterday."

Her eyes glinted and a smirk formed at the corner of her mouth. "I vomited on the shuttle yesterday."

"Oh yeah?" I said. This girl had obvious memory and . . . *conversational* issues, and I had stuff to think about. So I started walking faster.

"Yes. But I feel better today."

"Mm-hmm," I said, staring straight ahead.

"Are you excited about class?"

Man. Would this girl never shut up? I kept walking.

"I'm pretty jazzed. I bet we get to learn a bevy of fascinating space facts."

I looked at her like "You have got to be kidding me."

"Plus," she said, leaning her pale face toward mine and grabbing my arm to stop me, "I can tell you what the blue light is. And the humming. I know all about the humming."

10

I stared at Larc, gaping. How did she know about the blue light? And more importantly, how did she know that *I* knew about the blue light?

She smiled at me, flashing those teeth mottled with blue braces. I yanked my arm from her grip and kept walking. I wasn't sure I wanted to delve into taboo subjects with this girl. I couldn't tell if she was setting me up for some kind of practical joke or what. Kids were always causing me grief, and sometimes it seemed like the girls were the worst. At least with the boys, I *knew* when they wanted to come after me. But with girls, well, they were trickier. They'd smile at you kind of pretty and lure you in. Then *whap*. Someone would drop a grasshrinker in your pants and you'd spend the next three hours in the nurse's office waiting to resize.

"Don't you want to know what I know?" asked Larc in a singsong voice.

"No," I growled, even though I was dying to find out what she knew.

"Fine," she said, and walked ahead of me, her white ponytail bouncing from side to side.

I slumped my shoulders and grumbled to myself. Should I be nice to this girl? It didn't *seem* like she wanted to be mean to me. But really, was it even that important for me to figure out what was in the hallway? It was probably something stupid. But if it was something stupid, why did it have that crazy net? And why did I get into so much trouble?

I quickened my pace to catch up to Larc. Without looking her straight in the face, I saw with a sideways glance that she was smirking.

"Okay," I said in a low voice, with a little more attitude than I intended, "what about the blue light and the humming and—"

She cut me off with an excited whisper. "It's an escape pod."

I frowned. "So? There's an escape pod right by my apartment. There's nothing exciting about that."

"No, dummy, it's a special escape pod, with faster thrusters *and* search-and-rescue capabilities."

My shoulder rose in a kind of half shrug and I said, "I still don't get it. If it's an escape pod, it shouldn't be a secret. People have to know where the escape pods are, duh. Plus, the pod by my apartment doesn't have a blue glow and it doesn't make any noise. I think you're just making this up."

She grinned and hoisted her backpack farther up on her shoulder. "Oh, I'm not making it up."

"How do you even know that I was over there?"

"I saw you and your dad coming out of the hall-way." She laughed. "Boy, he looked furious."

"You saw us?" I asked. "But Dad looked all around. . . . There was no one within a mile of us."

"He didn't look up, did he? I was coming back from the cafeteria with some doughnuts for my dad when I saw you guys down in the lobby. I would have brought some doughnuts back for my mom, too, but I don't have a mom. Maybe sometime I can bring doughnuts to you and your dad. And your mom."

I had to figure this girl out. She wasn't like any girl I'd ever met before. I couldn't decide if she was kidding me or if she was genuinely trying to be helpful. She had this spark in her eye like she was totally in control of the situation (and yet totally joking around at the same time). And she acted like we'd been best friends for years. I didn't even know anything about her!

"Anyway, the escape pod by your apartment doesn't run on plasma propulsion," she said, stopping just out-side the classroom door.

"What?"

"Plasma propulsion. That's why the hidden pod glows blue and makes a humming noise. It's the magnets. That's also why the pod is so far down a hallway. It has to be away from the captain's controls or the magnets will interfere with all of the instruments."

"But that's ridiculous," I argued, remembering possibly the only thing I learned in astrophysics. "Plasma propulsion is what makes ships able to travel far out into the universe. An escape pod would never need that kind of power unless . . ." I trailed off.

"Unless it was going to be launched into—or from—deep space."

"But the *Sojourner*'s pods are only meant to be short-range. That way if we have to escape for some reason, people won't get lost and it'll be easier to rescue everyone. That's what my mom said, at least."

Larc raised her eyebrows in a way that made my stomach drop. Then she opened the classroom door. There were already several kids sitting at desks and rustling their stuff.

"Who *are* you?" I asked as she chose a desk in the front of the classroom.

"I told you, my name is Larc."

"Right. But where are you from? You're not from Star City. I would have seen you in school. And how do you know all this stuff?" I sat down at the desk behind her.

She turned in her seat and said, "One: I *am* from Star City. I was, uh, homeschooled by my nanny."

"Your *nanny*?" I said.

"Natalie Jones. The nicest lady on the planet."

"Hang on. Isn't Natalie Jones the name of the park out by the Project airfield? It is. Natalie Jones Park. I airboard at Jones Park all the time."

Larc blinked a couple of times and acted like she hadn't heard me. "And two: I *know* stuff because my dad works on a lot of special projects. He's the most skilled astrorobotics employee the Project has." She drew circles on my desk with her finger. "Plus, I'm a good listener. People tend to not notice when I'm in a room, and, well, they chat."

"Not notice you? Yeah, right." I didn't mean it as a compliment. This was the freakiest girl—person, really—I had ever met. She was probably two feet taller than me; her hair was crazy white, her skin almost translucent. And those blue braces . . . Plus the supposedly one-size-fits-all jumpsuit she wore was way too short. I could see the tops of her Project-issued socks and a blindingly white patch of skin on each of her legs.

I furrowed my brow and bent down to grab my handheld from my bag.

I froze.

At that moment I caught a whiff of something very familiar. Something I thought I'd never smell again: the commingling of burnt coffee beans and sweet old-lady perfume.

I closed my eyes, hoping that I was just imagining things, until I heard . . .

"Sleeping, Mr. Stellar? Not a great way to start off your first day in class."

My eyes shot open and so did my mouth. What was *Mrs. Halebopp* doing here?

**"Your original teacher** was unable to make the trip," Mrs. Halebopp said in her gravelly voice. "I was called in at the last minute. For those of you who don't know me, my name is Mrs. Halebopp." She paused and ran her fat gray tongue over her lips. "I'll be your teacher for the duration of this trip." She shot me a smirk.

I thought I was going to faint. Or throw up. Or throw up and then faint. Up until that moment the only thing this trip had going for it was that I never had to find myself in Mrs. H's clutches ever again. But here she was, leaning over my desk, her snarled beehive blocking out the light, just like she'd been doing every school day all year.

"I hope you've been working on your speech, Mike."

I gripped my desk and looked into her bottomless eyes. "Well, uh, to be honest, I . . ."

"Didn't think you were going to have to finish it after all, did you?" She cackled. "Well, look on the bright side. It's going to be a new assignment for this class, which means you'll have a leg up. Of course, I'll grade you harder because you've had more time for research, and I'll expect your speech to be longer—and given earlier—than everyone else's, but . . ." She trailed off.

I didn't know what to say. I closed my eyes and tried to wish her away.

Mrs. Halebopp swept herself over to the holoboard hanging in the front of the classroom, leaving me in a wake of burnt coffee stench. She began writing the rules for the assignment, which by this time I had memorized.

Larc turned around in her seat and whispered, "I think she likes you."

I stared at my handheld, not wanting to get caught whispering.

"Seriously," said Larc, braces glinting. "I've never seen her take such a liking to—"

"What do you mean you've 'never seen her'?" I blurted out in a fierce whisper. "You were homeschooled, remember?"

Larc sucked in her bottom lip, smiling. She turned

back around in her seat. And before I could even try to figure out what Larc was hinting at, Mrs. Halebopp winked and motioned for her to go to the big teacher's desk at the front of the room.

I had never, ever seen Mrs. Halebopp wink. The sight frightened and captivated me. I thought I could actually hear rusty creaking coming from her eyelid.

Larc flounced out of her seat. I stared after her in disbelief. She and Mrs. H held a short private conversation and then Larc returned to her seat. I tapped her on the shoulder.

"What was that all about?" I whispered.

"Wouldn't you like to know?" she singsonged over her shoulder.

I glanced up at Mrs. H hulking behind her desk. Seeing that she was shuffling some papers and not looking at the class, I leaned forward and whispered to Larc. "Do you know her or something?"

Without turning around, Larc just shrugged. Then Mrs. H was up, passing some kind of awful pop quiz to the class.

"Though I have all of your records, I'd like to see how you do on this quiz. It will help me understand what level I should begin teaching on. Beginner . . ." And here she looked squarely at me. "Or advanced." She looked at Larc with a smile. "Write out a timeline of Venus Aldrin's greatest accomplishments. You have ten minutes."

She paced the aisles to make sure no one was cheating and she seemed to pause for an extended amount of time by my desk. I hurriedly began working on my quiz.

*2150—Venus Aldrin hired by the Project*

*2157—Venus Aldrin creates Search and Rescue Department after third-generation Mercury probe is lost*

*2162—Venus Aldrin eats a sandwich*

*2163—Venus Aldrin takes a nap*

Finally I heard Mrs. H's green shoes click forward to Larc's desk. She leaned over to Larc and said, "I know this is probably very simple for you, honey, but just play along. I'll add something challenging to your presentation assignment."

*Honey?*

"Okay, Aunt Beebo. I'm excited to see what you've chosen for me to research!" Larc whispered enthusiastically.

*Aunt Beebo?*

Oh, holy mother of donkeys. Mrs. Halebopp was Larc's aunt!

I practically fell out of my desk. Mrs. H turned around and looked at me with a grimace.

"I, uh . . ." I swallowed. "I'm feeling very, suddenly,

tremendously like I'm going to spew chunks. Please, may I be excused?"

Mrs. H grunted. "It's coming out of your quiz time."

"Fine." I scrambled to my feet and bolted out the door. I saw a men's restroom and staggered inside. At the sinks I splashed cold water on my face and looked into the mirror.

I ducked into a stall at the farthest end of the restroom and plucked the peapod from my pocket. "Mrs. H is Larc's aunt," I said to myself in disbelief. "I have *got* to talk to Stinky."

"**That is not** just fishy, Mike. That is *funkified* fishy."

Stinky's voice was crackly through the peapod as I relayed all the morning's craziness.

"Am I a nutbar to think something bizarre is going on? Am I turning into a conspiracy freak or something?"

"It definitely sounds like something weird is happening, Mike. I'm not sure about the escape pod, but the Mrs. H thing is definitely bizarro. And that Sugar Bear guy? *He's* the nutbar."

"I know! I don't know what that guy is up to. And Mrs. H! She doesn't even work at the Project and suddenly she's a teacher on board *my* ship? She has a mystery niece who's our age but never came to school? That's deep-sea fishy."

"Do you think you can find out what's up with her?" Stinky asked.

"Who? Mrs. H? How can I find anything out? Good grief, at this point she probably has my brain waves downloading into her handheld."

Stinky made an exasperated noise that sounded like a balloon deflating. "You're the one on the ship with her, doof. What am *I* supposed to do?"

"Dude. That's exactly right. *I'm on a ship*. How am I supposed to snoop around and find out why Mrs. H is here? It's not like I can fake my eyeball scan and bust into her apartment or anything." But as I said that, I wondered if finding out more about Mrs. H would be as hard as I thought.

"What if you ask the kids at school if they've ever heard of this Larc girl, Stink? She had to have left her house at some point," I said. "Maybe kids at the library know her or something."

"I'll ask around, but I can't promise I'll come up with anything," Stinky said unconvincingly. "And I'm not talking to any *teachers,* that's for sure." He paused. "What's Larc's last name, anyway?"

"I don't know, man. Probably Halebopp. I mean, the girl is on the ship with her dad, who's pretty tall and ugly, so he's probably Mrs. H's brother." I shivered to even think about that vile woman having relatives.

"What about Larc's mom?" Stinky asked.

"She said she doesn't have a mom."

We were both quiet for a few seconds and suddenly it was as if angels from Uranus had sent me a vision. I let out a bwa-ha-ha-ha-I-have-a-plan laugh. "I have a brilliant idea, Stinky!"

"What?" he asked slowly.

"Detention!"

"What do you mean 'detention'?"

"You can cause trouble in class—throw a flash-nobang or something. That'll get you a detention for sure. Then, if you get lucky, you'll have to e-file papers and stuff in Mrs. H's old office. You'll be able to snoop around—in the lion's den!" I was suddenly very excited (and a little bit jealous) about Stinky's new top-secret mission.

Stinky was more skeptical. "But why would Mrs. H have anything about Larc in her office?"

"I'm not talking about Larc, man. I'm talking about Mrs. H. Maybe you can find out what she's doing on the ship."

"I don't know, Mike," Stinky said, and I thought I could actually hear him shaking his head. "Detention? The substitute teacher is almost as pure evil as Mrs. H. And if I get another detention, my mom is going to fry my—"

"I don't think it could hurt to see what's there." I pouted.

"Fine. But don't get mad when I can't find anything. Seriously, Mike, if there really is some kind of conspiracy going on, you can't expect to find clues just laying around in people's abandoned hard drives."

"Mother of donkeys, Stinky, do you want to help me or not?"

Neither one of us said anything for a while. "Mother of donkeys" had been one of Hubble's favorite phrases, and since he'd disappeared, things could get a little awkward when one of us accidentally uttered it.

Finally Stinky spoke up.

"What does Nita think about all of this? Surely she's noticed your parents acting weird. Did you tell her about the escape pod? I guess she probably doesn't know about Mrs. H yet."

"Oh, *man*," I said loudly, and grimaced, trying to keep my voice lower. "I totally forgot to tell you. Nita isn't even here!"

"*What?!*"

"She didn't pass the security clearance. She's moving in with Gram."

Stinky made a *sheeeeew* noise and said, "Mike, that is one important detail you left out."

I didn't say anything, because there was another important detail I'd left out, too.

Stinky continued. "Maybe I should find her and tell her about everything."

I bit my lip and then just started talking before I chickened out. "The thing is, Stink, she was talking really strangely when I saw her last."

"What do you mean?"

"I mean, if you go talk to her, she may just upset you."

"What are you babbling about, boogermunch? Out with it."

As quickly as I could, I mumbled, "Whenshehugged megoodbyeshetoldmetohelpherfindHubble."

"What?" Stinky's voice faded into a kind of whisper. "Hubble?"

"I know, man. She told me to watch out for anything weird and to help her try to find him."

"Well, but . . . that's impossible. Isn't it?" Stinky's voice sounded like it had the only time he'd gotten punched in the stomach. (Marcy Fartsy, fourth grade.) It had been really hard for him to lose his older brother, and even harder to know that his best friend's parents might be the reason. Stinky and I had made it through all the weirdness because Hubble had been like a brother to me, too. Hubble had been my go-to guy for questions and advice and everything. Losing him had hurt me almost as much as it had hurt Stinky. Our shared hurt is what had kept our friendship from becoming strained when Hubble vanished.

"So what is Nita talking about?" Stinky asked. "Do you think she knows something?"

"I can't imagine she'd know anything more than we do."

"I don't know, Mike. I bet she does." Stinky's voice was stronger now; he sounded more like himself. "I'm going to have to call her."

I made an exasperated noise.

"Look, I know that nowadays you and Nita want to eat each other for lunch," Stinky sighed, "but don't you think, maybe, possibly, she'd want to know that you guys made it safely to the ship?"

"I guess. . . ."

"Shut it." Stinky switched to his lawyery voice, so I knew he wanted to make a point. "You don't think that after twenty-four hours with your gram out there in Old Lady-ville, Nita'll be ready for a little news? You don't think she's tired of cooking biscuits and knitting and doing whatever else grandmas do all day?"

"What are you talking about, Stink? My gram's a police officer. You know that."

"Oh. Right. But you get my point, don't you?"

"Well, I'm not gonna. I'm not even supposed to have this peapod. Something about it interfering with the ship's instruments," I said. "But if you feel like you have to, find Nita. Tell her we're all skipping down the hallways and eating chocolate truffles all day. And that I have my own bathroom."

"Is her number still the same? I have it in one of Hubble's old handhelds. . . ."

"I guess it should be the same," I said.

"When do we rendezvous next?" Stinky asked.

I snorted, " 'Rendezvous'?"

He ignored me. "Want to say this time tomorrow?"

"Make it lunchtime. Then I won't have to sneak out of class."

"Right. Well. I'll talk to you tomorrow, then," Stinky said.

"Okay, Stink. Good luck with the detention." I snickered.

"Good luck to you, too. And if Mrs. Halebopp tries to eat you, Mike, go for her black eyeballs. Just jab at 'em with your fingers. That's what you're supposed to do with an alligator."

"It is not."

"Hey, it's one of the last things Hubble ever taught me. He saw it on the Extinct Animal Channel."

I laughed. "He was such a dork. Just like you." I paused suddenly, wondering if I shouldn't have said that. But Stinky was laughing, too.

"Bye, Mike."

"Bye, Stink."

I slipped the peapod back in my pocket and prepared to head back to class. Then I had a thought.

When would I have a better time to sneak back to the hallway to try and get a look at the escape pod again? Now was the perfect opportunity.

My heart pounded. My palms started sweating. I felt like I was about to go on a secret CIA operation. My mission was to discover all I could about the escape pod, and to do it before Mrs. H sent someone to find me. My conversation with Stinky had emboldened me. I was a new Mike. A Mike with a mission (instead of a Mike with a nagging curiosity that often got him grounded). I was going to find out the truth about what was going on. . . . I had nerves of steel. Nerves of steel!

I headed out of the bathroom with my collar up and my chin tucked down. I was embracing my new CIA self. I was preparing for my "infiltrate weird hallway" mission. I was crashing headlong into a kid in front of me.

I stepped off the kid's heels and looked up. I had exited the bathroom into a throng of kids from my class. They thundered past me toward some unknown destination. A couple of kids glanced at me and whispered to their friends, then hurried away as if I had sprouted oozing sores or something. Awesome.

"Lunchtime!" Larc hollered at me from the doorway of the classroom. I sighed and smoothed my collar back down. Larc came up and linked her arm with mine. So much for infiltrating the weird. The weird was now infiltrating me.

"Don't mind the lemmings. Just get out of their way. I'll help you make it to the cafeteria without being stomped to death." She started to lead me away from the spot my feet had frozen to. "You weren't really vomiting in there, were you, Michael?"

I yanked my arm away from her. "None of your business. And don't call me Michael." So much for cozying up.

"Well, I hope you weren't, because we're having cheeseburgers for lunch today. Real meat." She smacked her lips and widened her eyes like she was some kind of starved animal. "There's only two weeks' worth of real meat on the ship and then it'll all be soy patties. I hope you're feeling carnivorous." She walked backward so she could look at me and talk at the same time.

"Why don't you turn around?" I said snarkily. "You're going to fall on your butt."

"Mr. Stellar!"

*Argh.*

"Nice of you to finally rejoin us."

"What? Was I gone very long?" I spluttered, playing dumb.

"One-hour detention after class to think about it."

I looked up at the metal bulk of the ship's ceiling and exhaled slowly so I wouldn't say something I'd truly regret.

"Tough luck, Mr. Stellar," Larc said, turning around and walking by my side. "Detention on the first day of class. I bet your parents are going to be cah-raaazy mad at you." She screamed the "raaazy" part like she was an opera singer.

"Larc!" Mrs. Halebopp's voice rumbled back toward us and I shot a ha-ha-you're-in-trouble look at Larc.

"I'm disappointed in you. Screaming down the hallway is inappropriate—*and* not very mature, is it? One-hour detention for you, too."

For the first time Larc's smile faded.

"Ha-ha," I said. "Now your dad is going to be crazy mad, too." But I didn't sing it.

Larc was sullen until we reached the cafeteria door. Then she brightened.

"You save us a table and I'll go get the food."

"B-but—" I stammered. Before I could explain that I wanted to be alone, she had disappeared into the lunch line.

Not feeling up for a fight, I decided not to go chasing after her. I settled into a hard plastic chair and crossed my legs, resting my foot on the edge of the table. I thought about the conversation I'd just had with Stinky. I was going to have to snap into action. I needed to practice some of the latest hacking techniques, not to mention investigate the so-called personal homework station in my room. I wondered if it was a stand-alone computer system or if it was networked or what. I was going to have to dust off my research skills, too.

I buried my face in my hands. What I really needed to do was concentrate on my presentation and just ignore all this other stuff. Then I laughed to myself. Yeah, right.

"What are you laughing about?" Larc dropped a tray of food onto the table. "Dig in."

I reached for a cheeseburger. Larc was looking at me expectantly.

"Uh, cheers," I said, holding my burger up to smack with hers. She took the other burger off the tray and plopped it down in front of her. She did not return my cheers.

I shrugged. "Whatever."

Larc stared at me from across the table. Her arms were folded in front of her and she peered at me like I was a monkey at the zoo.

"What?" I asked.

"You're a very interesting person, Mike Stellar."

I shrugged again. The cheeseburger really was pretty good. And she had brought me some fries, too.

"I on't oh how shoo ansher at," I said with my mouth full. I was starting to feel a little uncomfortable.

"I think you like my company but don't want to admit it."

I didn't say anything.

"I think I intrigue you." She said "intreeeeeg" and raised her eyebrows at me.

"Who said anything about you intreeeeeging me?" I retorted, my face flushing. "Maybe I just feel sorry for you because everyone else thinks you're a freak."

Larc wasn't fazed. "Maybe you like me because I'm more of a freak than you."

I snatched up my burger and stood as if I was going to stomp off to another table. But there weren't any other tables to go to, so I sat back down in a huff.

"Maybe you like me because I'm the only person who likes you." Larc was talking softly now, unperturbed, leaning her face toward me.

I crossed my arms angrily. "I don't know what you're talking about."

"Tell me why people whisper when you walk down the hall, Mike."

"Like you don't already know," I muttered, feeling my appetite drain away.

"I *don't* know. I told you, I was homeschooled."

I looked at her incredulously. "You mean to tell me you don't know anything about the *Spirit*? About my parents? Do you have *eyeballs*? Do you have *ears*? Did you not see the black ribbons on all of the trees for like six months? Did you not hear the church bells every time there was a memorial service?" I was breaking into a sweat.

"Uh-uh. What happened?"

I took a sip from the water pouch she'd brought me with my lunch. "I'm just giving you the short version, okay? I don't really like to talk about it."

"Fine," she said, looking very serious for once.

I took another sip of my drink and lowered my voice. "Almost two years ago, during the first Mars mission, there was some kind of miscalculation with the thickness of the ship's metal hull. The hull has to be a certain thickness to make it safely through a Fold. But when the *Spirit* went through the Mars Fold, it never came out the other side. The scientists at the Project said the hull probably crumbled and the ship just disintegrated. Kablooey. The pressure indicators and magnetic indicators on the ship were shooting back crazy numbers right before the Project lost contact. That's where the disintegration idea comes from."

I fiddled with my drink and thought about ending the conversation, but something made me keep talking. It actually felt kind of good.

"I've always secretly hoped that the ship made it through the Fold just fine," I continued. "Maybe their radios were just messed up from the Fold. I asked my mom about that once and she said there's like a two percent chance of me being right. But still. Two percent— at least it's something. Better than I did on my last astrophysics test."

Larc laughed softly and said, "I can help you with astrophysics if you want."

I shook my head.

"So why did this tragedy make people hate you?"

"During the investigation it came out that my mom was in charge of the group who calculated the thickness of the *Spirit*'s hull. And both Mom and Dad had specifically requested not to be members of the flying crew on the mission."

Larc's white eyebrows furrowed.

"It looked like my parents had been part of a plan to ruin the mission. And the public cried for a trial, but there never was one."

"Why not?"

"Because they had nothing to do with it!" I said sharply. "They *weren't guilty!* How *could* they have been? They're my *parents!*" Some kids from the next table turned and looked at us.

"But what about the calculations? What about the request to stay on Earth?"

I started to answer her, but a loud ping sounded in the room and everyone started gathering their things. Larc and I stayed in our seats until Mrs. Halebopp came by.

"Don't dally now, children. We have an afternoon of research ahead of us."

I scowled and stood up. Mrs. H lumbered away.

Larc shook her head. "Don't mind her. Her bark is worse than her bite."

"She's bitten you?" I asked, only half joking. "I hope you had your rabies shot."

Larc looked down at my tray as I scooped it off the table. "You didn't finish your burger."

"Neither did you," I said, pointing at her burger. It didn't even have one bite taken out of it. "Maybe you should get a doggie bag."

"I'm not hungry. And I don't have a dog."

"Ha-ha," I said as I dumped the food into the de-atomizer.

"What?"

We filed out of the cafeteria behind the rest of the class, with Mrs. Halebopp shooing us out the door.

"You're sure your parents aren't guilty?" Larc whispered to me.

"Of course I'm sure," I said through clenched teeth. But to be honest, I wasn't really sure about anything anymore.

14

I headed out of the cafeteria and told Larc I had to go to the bathroom. Instead of going to the bathroom, though, I slithered my way back to the tiny hallway that led to the escape pod. I darted around corners and hid behind benches, afraid that someone would spot me outside class. When I finally got to the hallway, I was shocked to find it completely closed. The bench was gone and now there was a door—with no doorknob—and a glowing keypad.

Hmmmm.

This put a wrench into my "find out everything I can as quickly as I can" plan. For a second I thought about randomly banging on the keypad, but that didn't seem like a good idea. Maybe I could hack it. I stepped closer and examined the device until I heard quick footsteps coming up behind me. I darted away from the doorway and crouched behind a nearby bench. It was a terrible hiding place but it was as good as I could do.

Breathing hard, I concentrated on willing myself to become invisible. Mr. Shugabert walked past me and stopped in front of the keypad. What was an executive assistant doing in front of a secret hallway? He paused for a second and I thought, *Oh, man, I'm toast!* But then I heard a rustle and some quick beeps. I barely stuck my head out from behind the bench and I saw Mr. Shugabert slipping a handheld into his pocket as the hallway door whooshed open and he walked into the narrow passageway. The door whooshed shut behind him and I stood up.

Well, that was that. I steadied myself and started toward class. No need to hack the keypad; I just needed to get my hands on Sugar Bear's spankin' cool handheld. And figure out what on earth he was up to.

Before I got two feet closer to the classroom door, I felt my peapod shake in my pocket.

Stinky was breathless. He didn't even let me finish answering. He shouted, "Nita isn't with your gram!"

"What?"

"She's not there, Mike. I ducked out of class and called your gram as soon as I found her number. She was totally freaked. She's been trying to contact your parents since the shuttle took off. The Project shipped

Nita's clothes and stuff to your gram's house but that was it. Nita never showed up."

"Whoa, whoa. Slow down," I said, sinking onto a bench. "What do you mean Gram's been trying to contact my parents? There's an emergency contact number that relatives are given."

"Dude, the number doesn't work. It's bogus. Your gram says she's getting an 'all circuits busy' message."

"*What?*"

"She's filed a missing persons report on Nita. She said that she was going to file a report on the whole family if she couldn't contact you guys on the ship. I told her I had talked to you and I think that made her feel a little better."

"I don't understand why she can't contact the ship. Hasn't she talked to anyone at the Project?"

"Of course she has, Mike," Stinky said impatiently, "but she says they're not being very helpful. She had to threaten them with police action before they finally gave in and let her speak to some lady in charge."

I stared at the hologram of the solar system circling above my head. "Well, we have to find Nita," I said, more to myself than to Stinky.

"Duh," Stinky said. "Your gram has the whole police department behind her."

"I know, I know," I said impatiently, "but *we* should try to find her, too. Maybe she just ran away. Maybe this has something to do with the Hubble stuff she was talking about before. . . ."

My brain was whirling and the only thing I could think of to tell Stink about was Mr. Shugabert and the keypad.

"Well, be careful, whatever you do," Stinky said. "You don't want this Sugar Bear guy to—"

"Hey, Stinky," I interrupted. Something about his voice had just changed. "Talk again."

"What do you mean?"

"Say anything."

"Anything."

"Your voice is coming in clearer than it was before."

"Hunh." Stinky sounded clearer but not impressed.

"I mean, you sound like you're right around the corner instead of . . ." I turned and looked up at the front of the lobby, through the giant front window.

Stinky had started describing his plan to call the Project himself when I interrupted him.

"The ship is moving."

"What do you mean moving?"

"It's traveling through space. The stars are all streaking by, and the Earth is . . ." I was puzzled. "The Earth is getting *closer*."

"It's way too early for you guys to be on the move," Stinky said.

"I know. Mom said there's at least two weeks of

work just getting supplies off of SpacePort and onto the ship. Plus, we need another week to power up the plasma-propulsion units." I stood up from the bench and paced back and forth. "It doesn't make any sense. Why would we be on the move so early?"

I stopped pacing and looked at the little timer on my peapod. "Listen. I'm sorry, but I really have to go. I've been away from class so long now Mrs. H is going to give me detention for a week."

"Well, I'm gonna go call your gram back."

"Let her know I'm telling Mom and Dad about Nita—and that we're all fine on the ship."

"Hey, Mike?"

"Yeah?"

"You know they're—we're—going to find Nita, right?"

"Yeah. I know."

"Okay, man. Bye."

"Bye."

I sprinted back to class, but when I got to the door, I thought, *This is stupid. Nita is lost back on Earth and Gram is freaking out.* I didn't care about getting a million detentions. I needed to go find Mom and Dad.

**Other than being** really mad at me for breaking the rules and talking to Stinky via peapod, Mom and Dad seemed to take the news that Nita was missing remarkably well. They seemed upset but . . . preoccupied.

We were in a tiny room in the back of the ship. It was called a Family Room and was designed for private contact with Earth if someone had news of a family catastrophe. (None of our private quarters had communicators that could reach Earth.) The walls were a kind of rosy color and the floor had soft beige carpet. Mom and I were sitting on a plush blue sofa and Dad was pacing back and forth in front of a small table where the communicator was embedded.

As Dad talked to Gram, he described the clothes Nita had been wearing and the mole she has on her left shoulder. Mom would shout out something irrelevant every now and then, like "Don't forget she just had a haircut," and then go back to frantically writing on her handheld. It was all very surreal.

"What are you doing?" I asked finally, not understanding why Mom was so concerned with her handheld and so *not* concerned with helping Dad give an accurate description of her missing daughter.

"I can't really talk about it, Mike. The flight schedule has been pushed up, that's all. A lot of things are going on right now." She talked to me without even looking up.

"The ship is moving," I said. "We're leaving too early for the Fold, aren't we?"

Mom stopped tapping on her handheld and looked at me. Her eyes looked a little crazy, but everything else about her was perfectly in place. She set her handheld down and put her hand on my knee.

"Yes. The timetable has been moved forward. But that's nothing for you to worry about, okay?"

"But what about the plasma propulsion? We haven't had time to generate the power, or . . ."

She smiled wearily at me and then gave me a spontaneous hug. "I hate that I forget how smart you are sometimes."

"What is *that* supposed to mean?" I asked, somehow feeling offended and proud at the same time. People always acted like I was a big dummy, but before . . . everything happened . . . I'd had the highest grades in my class. At least Mom never forgot that—no matter how annoying her nagging was.

"I just mean that with all of your detentions and poor grades . . . Well, I wish you could think of a different way to act out, Mike. You're just too smart to waste your education by trying to get back at me and Daddy."

"Get *back* at you? For what?"

"For everything, Mike. For all of the unwanted attention our family has received. For Hubble." She looked at me intently. "I know you're still very angry with us."

"I am not. I don't even think about it anymore," I lied.

"Oh, you don't? Hubble was like a big brother to you, Mike. I know you miss him—and now Nita, too. And I know being on this ship must be creating a lot of confusing feelings for you."

"I'm not confused!" I shouted, standing up. "I just don't know what to think. I know that Hubble's gone and now Nita is gone. And the ship is moving too soon for us to survive a trip through the Fold and . . . and it seems like the *Spirit* stuff is all happening again." I stopped myself, knowing that I'd just accidentally proven her point.

There was silence in the room. Dad was listening intently to Mom and me. He was doing his typical doctor thing—observe the situation, then assess, and soon he'd be offering his "cure." To him everything was like an illness—a problem with a solution. A blister and a bandage.

"I'm here to keep you safe," Mom said in a low voice. "It's my job to keep *everyone* safe. Let *me* worry about the plasma propulsion. Let *me* worry about the Fold."

"What about Nita?"

"I'm sure she's fine," Mom said.

"How do you know?" I shouted. "Gram is *freaking out*."

Dad sighed. "Nita is nearly an adult, Mike. She can make her own decisions now. Her staying with Gram, well, that was something she was supposed to do. But as we all know, people don't always do what they're supposed to do." He and Mom exchanged looks.

"What Daddy is saying, Mike, is to trust us. Trust Nita. Everything will be fine."

I didn't understand any of this. They seemed so . . . calm. What was going on here? Mom was tapping away at her handheld again.

"Well, I better get back to class. I have a detention," I said, still irritated by Mom's preoccupation with that stupid handheld and by the idea of zipping, unprepared, through a Fold that might eat us just like it ate the *Spirit*. "Plus, I really have to get my speech researched. At least in detention I'll have some quiet time to work. Don't want anyone thinking I'm a moron when I present my speech." I gave Mom the stink eye.

I wanted out of the Family Room. Mom and Dad were smothering me and yet still keeping me at a distance. Though I would never admit it, I could understand why Mom and Dad weren't spazzing out about Nita's disappearance. I didn't really feel crazy worried about her, either.

I knew she'd have no trouble out on her own. Plus, her left hook is so quick no one would have enough strength or stamina to kidnap her. She must have run off somewhere. I hoped this was true. Why didn't we just call the EFEs and see if Nita was there? I was going to suggest this, but before I could say anything, Mr. Shugabert opened the door and stuck his head into the room.

"Everything okay in here?" he asked, not smiling for once.

"We're fine, Leslie," Dad answered. His words said, "We're fine," but their tone said, "Leave us alone."

Instead of leaving, Mr. Shugabert opened the door a little more and stepped one foot into the room. "Would you like an escort back to class, Mike?"

"I'll take him," Dad said, coming up next to me and draping his arm over my shoulder.

Mr. Shugabert crossed his arms and smiled that crocodile grin of his. "I'm just trying to do my job, Al."

I heard my dad grit his teeth. He hated being called Al. He said it made him sound like an old man.

"I appreciate your concern," Dad said slowly. "But Mike and I are just on our way out."

Mom hugged and kissed me and hugged Dad, too, and then we pushed past Mr. Shugabert's hulking presence without another word. It was hard to place the weird vibe between Sugar Bear and Dad. It was like they were dogs sniffing each other's butts; would it lead to fighting or indifference?

Once we got a few yards away, I whispered to Dad, "What's the deal with that guy, anyway?"

"He's just trying to do his job," Dad said.

"Well, why didn't you let him?" I asked accusingly. "He's basically a glorified babysitter, right?"

"This is a time when we need to stick together as a family, Mike. I know you're feeling confused and scared about Nita's disappearance and I want you to know that you can always come to me or your mother if you need to express some of your feelings." Dad had pretty much ignored my question.

"He seems pushy to me," I said, pressing the point and ignoring Dad's little speech. "And he is *always* around."

Dad sighed. "That's what he's supposed to do. He's

here to take care of us, to lessen the load of everyday crap so that Mom and I can concentrate on our jobs."

I didn't say anything. We had made it back to the classroom. I held my hand out, palm forward, to wave it in front of the door opener, but Dad put his hand over mine.

"You know your mother and I love you very much, right, Mike?"

As much as I hated to admit it, it was nice to know he and Mom still realized I existed in the same world they did.

Finally I muttered, "I better get back to class."

Dad shrugged, suddenly looking really tired. "Well, come straight ho—to the apartment after class, then."

"I have a detention, remember?"

"Right," Dad said, crossing his arms. "Well, come home directly after your detention. Don't hang around in the hallways. Just get home."

"Fine," I said.

Without warning he grabbed me in a tight, awkward hug. I stood there, arms stiff at my sides. I tried to free my hands to hug him back, but they just sort of patted at his hips, which was embarrassing, so I stopped and just let him hug me. He didn't seem to mind. Finally he let go.

"Have fun in class, son."

"Yeah, okay."

"I'll come find you if we learn anything about your sister."

"Okay," I said again. I raised my palm to the door and waved it past the sensor. The door shot open and Mrs. Halebopp appeared, standing in front of the class. She shot me a look that said, "Well, come in or stay out, but don't stand in the doorway."

I swallowed hard and walked into the classroom. My brain was twisting, spinning, grappling to make sense of everything. I felt like I was losing my mind.

**"It looks like** you're losing your mind," Larc whispered to me as I sat down at my desk behind her.

"I'm having a very strange day," I said. I pulled my handheld out of my backpack and noticed the dreaded stench of burnt coffee beans hovering in my nostrils.

"Mr. Stellar," Mrs. Halebopp whispered fiercely. "I do believe you have broken the world record for longest walk back from lunch."

I started to stutter an excuse when she held up her hand.

"Your mother just buzzed down and informed me of your family situation." Her face contorted into what I could only guess was a sympathetic grimace. "We can postpone your detention for another day. However, I would still like you to work on your research project until the end of class today. If you would prefer to go to your apartment and study, you may."

I swallowed. Was she being *nice* to me?

"Okay," I said, shocked, and put my handheld back into my bag. I didn't really want to go back to my apartment, but I definitely didn't want to stay in class, either.

The monstrous blue hair teetered down in front of my face. "If you don't mind taking Larc with you, you can both study together."

"S-sure," I stammered. I figured Mrs. H wanted me to take Larc along so that she could vouch that I actually researched instead of goofing off.

"Oh, and, Mike?"

I looked up into those bottomless eyes. "Yes?"

"I trust you've had plenty of time to glean some pertinent quotes from the book I let you borrow?"

"Uh, of course." Dang! I hadn't even opened that dumb book yet.

"Excellent. May I have it back now?"

"Well . . . I don't really . . . It's not with me right now."

Mrs. H was still towering over me. Her crooked finger arched in front of my nose and pointed into my bag. "What's that, then?"

I looked to see what she was pointing at. "Oh. That's just a book my dad told me to have my teacher look

at—not you—the one who was *supposed* to be here."
My voice sounded very bitter—even to me.

"I'll take that book as collateral, then. You can have
it back when I get *my* book back."

I wasn't sure about giving Dad's book to Mrs. H. He
was going to want it back now that the original teacher
wasn't here for me to give it to. Unless . . . No! I tried to
banish the thought from my mind, but it wouldn't budge.
Did Dad *know* that Mrs. H was replacing the teacher?
Why wouldn't he have told me? And why would he want
her to have a *book*? It didn't make any sense. I took a deep
breath and pushed the thought of Dad and Mrs. H as
Weird Secret Book Collaborators out of my mind.

"Here," I said, handing over the book. "Can Larc
and I go now?"

Larc started gathering up her stuff and Mrs.
Halebopp said something to her quietly. She patted Larc
on the shoulder and then stalked over to another table
to yell at some boys for burning each other's hair with
modified laser pens.

"Ready?" Larc's blue braces glowed as she grinned
at me. "My project is on terraforming, too. We can help
each other out!"

"Great," I mumbled, and trudged out of the classroom. I could feel Larc behind me. She was so close on
my heels that when I stopped, she crashed into me.

She giggled and smoothed her jumpsuit as I turned

to face her. "You know, I really don't feel like going to my apartment right now," I said glumly.

"But we have to study," Larc said. "That's the only reason Aunt Beebo let us out of class. So that we could study together and I could help you."

"Yeah?" I said kind of roughly. "Help me? Well, your aunt Beebo is a psycho nutjob who is usually out to get me, so excuse me if I'm just glad to be out of her sight."

Larc put her hand on my shoulder. "Mike, she told me about your sister. She thinks you and I should study together because it will help take your mind off what's going on."

"Whatever," I said, and started walking again.

"Let's just go to my apartment, then," Larc called after me. "We can study just as well over there."

I ran through the options in my head.

1. Go back to class and tell Mrs. H thanks for being nice, but no thanks.

2. Go to my apartment and be accosted by Sugar Bear's "helpful" recordings.

3. Go to Larc's and study.

For the first time ever, studying seemed like the best option.

"Fine," I grumbled. "Let's go study at your place."

"Great!" she said, matching my stride. "We're almost there."

She was right. In about two minutes we were outside her apartment door and she swiped her flash key to unlock it.

"Why don't you use the eyeball scanner?" I asked. "I thought the flash keys were only for power emergencies. I didn't even get one."

"The scanner is broken," Larc said over her shoulder. "Come on in."

I followed her into the apartment. It was a lot like mine, but it was in shades of blue. There was an extra door on the far wall, but really, it was practically a replica of my place.

"The computer is over here," Larc said as she crossed the room. She hit a button on the wall and a desk slid up from the floor. It was in the place that the viserator was in my apartment. "I can enlarge the monitor if you'd like to sit on the sofa and study."

"Sure," I said, not really caring. My mind was going in about a hundred directions. Whether to sit on the sofa was not one of them.

I plopped down and Larc sat next to me. She had a remote mouse to navigate the screen.

"Hey, a remote," I said. "What, your executive assistant doesn't change all your channels and run your computer programs for you?"

Larc stared at me like my hair was on fire. "What are you talking about?"

"Just joking." I gave a halfhearted chuckle. "That stupid Sugar Bear is always around. I'm surprised he's not here right now, begging to write down notes we dictate."

"Mike Stellar, sometimes I think you're speaking a foreign language. Except that I can speak all of the other languages and I *still* don't understand what you're talking about."

"Right," I said, rolling my eyes. "You speak all of the other languages. . . ." I took my handheld out of my bag.

"Good idea. Let's get down to business." Larc started clicking the remote and a zillion pages popped up on the monitor. I turned on my handheld and got ready to sync it up. Something, though, grabbed my attention.

The remote reminded me of something. Remote. Remote. Was it the word that reminded me? The thing? What was it? I racked my brain to figure it out, but I got nothing.

"Do you already have a lot of this information?" Larc asked. "I know you've been working on your paper for a while now."

"Weeeeell," I said, scanning the zillion pages on the monitor, "I have pretty much all of this stuff. But I could add something on the long-term effects of terraforming. My stupid report needs to be a lot longer or your darling aunt Beebo is totally gonna flunk me."

"I researched the long-term effects of terraforming for fun a while back. Would you like to see my old notes?"

"You research for fun?"

"Sure," she said with a devious smirk. "Don't you?"

I sighed and shook my head. Obviously, this girl was nuts.

It was driving me crazy that I couldn't figure out what the remote was tickling in my memory. A person? A place? A thing? Argh.

"Anyway," she continued, oblivious to the fact that I wasn't really listening, "we're going to need more stuff than that to satisfy Aunt Beebo. . . . She's going to want a thorough blah blah blah . . ."

I could see Larc's mouth moving, but I'd stopped paying attention eight words before.

Finally I interrupted. "I guess we could talk about the Factory Approach. It's supposed to work pretty well. At least theoretically."

Larc raised her eyebrows. " 'Theoretically.' Woohoo. You *are* smart! So the Factory Approach sets up carbon dioxide–producing facilities on the planet's surface," she said. "The carbon dioxide warms up the atmosphere, melts any water that's there, and, voilà, you have an atmosphere that can support life."

"Yeah, but doesn't the theory posit that the factories might work too well and overpollute the environment?

Won't superfast terraforming methods be more likely to kill a planet?"

" 'Posit'?" Larc grinned. "That's an old-man word." She clicked the remote a couple of times and the screen filled with pictures of old dudes.

I readied myself to ignore her silly remote clicking and launch into a speech about rapid overpollution as the major reason why the Factory Approach was a terrible idea when I paused. The clicking of the remote . . .

Nita!

That was it!

That was what the remote reminded me of!

Nita's com-bracelet. It was this stupid, cheap thing that Hubble had bought her years before. It was *remotely* linked to the matching com-bracelet that he wore. She still wore hers, even though it didn't work. Well, it probably would have still worked with Hubble's matching com-bracelet, but . . . Anyway, that was it!

I jumped up from the sofa. Larc looked at me, startled. "What?" she asked. "Are there bugs in your pants?"

"No," I said, feeling silly for jumping up like that. "No. I'm cool." I sat back down, my mind racing.

Larc started talking and every now and then I nodded or grunted so that she would think I was paying attention. As she babbled I began scrolling crazily through my handheld. Stored somewhere on one of the hard drives was a hack I'd written ages ago when Stinky and I were trying to listen in on all the smoochy love talk between Nita and Hubble. It was a freakin' crazy awesome hack, because it had actually worked. Stinky and I just about died from alternately laughing and puking when we heard some of those love chats. If I could find the hack, I might be able to bust into Nita's com-bracelet again and hear what was going on around her.

My heart was beating at a totally unhealthy pace as I tapped the handheld screen furiously. The hack wasn't going to take very long, if I could just . . .

"Then all the planets will be dead," Larc was saying. "Right, Mike?"

"Wha? Dead planets? Uh, right," I answered, snapping to attention.

"Yes. . . . Well, that's the theory, anyway," Larc said, looking at me out of the corner of her eye. "Dead planets. Floating out in space."

"Hmmm?" I said.

"Are you paying attention to me, Michael Stellar? Your grade depends on this," Larc said, waving her hand in front of my eyes. I noticed a scary ugly scar on the palm of her hand. It was in a kind of star shape and had a big throbbing vein down the middle of it. It was the nastiest thing I'd seen in my entire life. But it was sort of cool, too.

"Ew, what's *that*?" I asked, grabbing for her hand.

"Mi-ike." Larc yanked her hand away and snapped

at me. "Focus. Have you heard anything I've been saying?"

"Right," I said. "Dead planets. Because the terra-forming can mess with the magnetism of the poles or something like that. I have it here." I motioned to my handheld.

"Cool. Can you shoot it to the monitor?"

"Oh, well, I'm kinda . . ."

Larc pounced at me, her icy eyes blazing, and tried to swipe my handheld. "I *knew* it, Michael Stellar! You're not studying at all, are you? You're playing some flight sim or something!"

"Whoa!" I hollered, hopping off the couch just in time to avoid her quick grab. Man, she was lightning fast. "I'm not playing games!" I shouted, dodging furniture as Larc chased me around the apartment. "I'm just . . . I'm working on a little side project right now. . . ."

"Side project?" Larc shrieked. "You're supposed to be studying. *We're* supposed to be studying. If my aunt Beebo knew that you were just fooling around—"

"I am most certainly *not* fooling around!" I shot back, jumping over the arm of the couch to get away from her. "I just remembered something about Nita, and I was try-ing to see if I could . . ." I realized I was shouting. And sweating. And standing on the couch. I took a deep breath and slid down, sinking into the cushion.

I quieted my voice. "I was trying to see if I could

contact her." I shook my head. "Well, not contact her, really, but listen in on her, wherever she is. I thought maybe I could—"

"Oh, Mike," Larc said, sitting next to me, her expression softening like someone had flipped a switch. "I know this has to be agonizing for you. I'm sorry I went crazy. Studying must be the last thing on your mind right now."

I scanned Larc's face with uncertainty. She was always so hard to read.

She leaned back into the sofa. "I don't know what I would do if my dad or my aunt Beebo ever went missing."

"You'd feel like a big pile of poo."

"Sorry?"

"That's how you'd feel. Like a big pile of poo."

Larc laughed and punched my shoulder. I pretended I was going to go schizoid and attack her, and she flinched.

"So are you writing a program or something? To find Nita?"

I told Larc what I was trying to do and she actually had a couple of helpful suggestions for things I could add to the hack—like a voice activator and a program that would allow me to sync my handheld's microphone up with Nita's com-bracelet.

For the rest of the afternoon, we worked on the

hack together and forgot about terraforming. It was kind of fun.

After a while I said, "Okay, let's test it out. I haven't calculated the distance from the ship to Nita yet, so we're gonna need to test on something within the ship, but at least that'll let us know if the core hack is working."

"Of course," Larc said. "What do you want to try it on?"

I looked around the room. "Let's see if we can use it to project our voices through the computer monitor. That'll be a good start."

I tapped a few commands into the handheld and we waited while everything calibrated. I held the microphone end up to Larc's face and said, "Say something."

"Something," she said, then smiled and stuck her tongue out at me. A few seconds later we heard her voice come through the TV loud and clear. We jumped up and I gave a happy hoot.

Then . . . something very weird happened.

The monitor talked back.

It said, "Did someone just . . . hoot?"

We glanced around the apartment, but no one was with us. The talking had definitely come from the monitor.

Larc pointed at it slowly.

The pages Larc had called up on the monitor were gone. In their place, the screen was divided into six sections. Each one looked like the living room of an apartment on the ship. In the bottom right-hand corner we could see two people sitting on a sofa. Larc and I got up off our sofa and peered more closely at the monitor. We were astonished to see ourselves staring at . . . ourselves.

"What the . . . ," I said, walking closer to the monitor. I saw my image in the bottom square walk toward the screen, too. My eyes widened and I carefully covered the microphone on my handheld with my palm. "It's like we're watching video surveillance," I whispered. "Our hack could never have done this. It wasn't sophisticated enough to—" I kept my hand over the microphone and with the other hand I tapped on my handheld's screen. Suddenly the images disappeared from the monitor and a map of the ship appeared. There were a handful of blinking dots moving down hallways and in and out of rooms.

"What is *that*?" Larc asked. I had no idea. I tapped my handheld screen and the surveillance-type video showed up again on the big monitor. I grabbed Larc's hand and dragged her behind the sofa. We crouched down, hiding, and peeked over the back of the sofa at the monitor.

"Is that your *dad*?" Larc asked.

Sure enough, in the top right square I saw Dad walk into a room and sit in a chair.

"Hey!" I said. "That's my apartment!"

Then Larc's dad walked into the room and sat down across from my dad on the sofa. Then I saw Mom appear, standing in the corner. There were figures appearing in all the boxes now.

"What are they doing?" Larc asked, her voice filled with wonder.

"I have no idea." My voice was not filled with wonder. It was starting to go hoarse with dread.

"Can they see us?"

"I don't know," I said. And then I added hopefully, "I don't think so."

Suddenly we could hear a lot of commotion. Someone said, "Hey. There it was again. Did you just hear a kid talk?" Larc and I looked at each other in horror and simultaneously looked at my handheld. My palm had slipped off the microphone and was now not-so-helpfully covering the On/Off button. Someone else said, "How could that be? This is a secure transmission." Then my mom said, "What the— Jim? Jim? Are you looking at the monitor? Why is the interface to your system turned on?"

"Uh, Larc," I said, turning to look at her.

"Yeah?"

"Looks like the hack works."

As Larc and I grabbed our stuff, we heard her dad say, "That's really strange. I thought I disabled my interface this morning when I knew I wouldn't be home for the meeting."

As we ran out of the apartment, I said, "Should we hide somewhere? Are they going to come after us?"

"You think they'll come looking for us?" Larc asked, not even out of breath.

I shrugged. "Why not? Two kids suddenly appear on some kind of weird closed-circuit camera thing? Not in school? Alone in an apartment in the middle of the day?" I flushed and dropped my eyes. "If you were a parent, what would you do?"

Larc ran her tongue over her glowing braces. "Were

you going to try to kiss me in there, Mike Stellar?" She didn't act scared or worried about being caught. She seemed to be enjoying herself immensely.

I abruptly stopped running. "*What?* Kiss you? No! Of course not! Why would I want to do tha—"

Suddenly we heard footsteps rounding the corner.

"In here!" Larc said, swiping her flash key and opening a door right next to us. She dragged me into the dark apartment. We both stood there for a minute, breathing hard and listening even harder. We didn't hear anything. My heartbeat began to calm down and I looked around. The apartment was dark but I could still see that it was pretty much the same as my apartment.

"Whose apartment is this?" I asked, picking up a small globe that was sitting on a shelf near the door.

"Aunt Beebo's."

I almost dropped the globe. *"Your aunt Beebo's?"* I felt my skin crawl as I realized I was standing in the lair of the devil. "Do you know what she would do if she knew I was in here?"

Larc offered, "She'd probably be relieved that you weren't getting pummeled by some insane person who was chasing you in the hallway."

"Relieved?" I laughed. "I wouldn't be surprised if your aunt Beebo *was* the crazy person chasing us in the hall."

"Don't be silly. She's teaching class, remember?" Larc wandered over to the kitchen and pushed a couple of buttons. "Do you want a drink or something?"

I wanted to say no, but then I thought a drink would actually be nice. "Okay," I grumbled, and Larc handed me a pouch of water.

She said, "Anything to eat? A snack or something? You didn't eat much for lunch."

I chuckled. "You're acting like my mother." Then I said quietly, "No, I don't want anything. Thanks, though."

It always seems dorky to say things that are polite to your friends. Why is that? I drank my water. . . . Hmm. Friends. Did I think of Larc as my friend? It still seemed like we hardly even knew each other.

Larc walked out of the kitchen and into the little living room. She sat on the sofa.

"We can still study, if you want."

I made a *pssssh* noise and waved my hand like I was backhanding a bug.

"What do you want to do, then?"

"Besides not get in trouble for hacking some internal system? Oh, I don't know. . . ." I gave Larc an exasperated look. "Play handball?"

She rolled her eyes at me. "Go study by your-self, then."

"How are you not worried about this?" I asked incredulously. "We just saw our parents and a bunch of other people on some secret internal surveillance system. *And they might have even seen us.* This doesn't bother you because . . . ?"

"Because nothing, Mike. If they were doing some kind of secret thing, they won't come after us."

"Why not?"

"Because, dope, if they come after us, they have to admit that *they* were doing something that obviously isn't protocol."

"Oh," I said. "Hmmm. That's a very good point."

Larc showed off her blue braces with a big smile. "So are we going to study or what?"

I wandered around the apartment, looking at odds and ends on the shelves lining the walls. There were old-fashioned poetry books and glowing knickknacks everywhere. I drank a sip of my water. After a bit of awkward silence, I said, "Has your dad been acting weird lately?"

Larc cocked her head to the side and said, "What do you mean?"

"I mean weird. Has he been acting secretive or whispery or anything? Does he raise his eyebrows a lot? Is he reading books?"

Larc raised *her* eyebrows and smiled in a joking way.

Then she said seriously, "I don't think so. I haven't seen any books around. And he's no weirder than usual. He always has classified projects he's working on for the Project. He doesn't talk about those. But I don't know if you'd call that being secretive. Why do you ask?"

I didn't know why I was opening up to this girl, but when I started talking, it was like white-water rapids. I couldn't have stopped even if I'd wanted to. By the time I finished, I'd told her practically everything. From Mom and Dad's acting so preoccupied, to Mr. Shugabert's creepy smile and knack for being everywhere, to Nita's strange request about Hubble . . . I just blurted it all out. And the whole time I talked, Larc sat on the sofa, looking thoughtful and never interrupting. Sometimes she played with her hair. Other times she wrinkled her lips over her teeth like she was trying to make sure her braces were still there. But she always kept her eyes on me and acted like she was taking everything in.

When I finished, I collapsed next to her on the sofa, dropping my empty water pouch on the floor. She got up and walked out of the room. A few minutes later she came back with a fresh water pouch and a candy bar. She handed them to me without saying anything.

"That was some story," she said finally. "I'd like to meet your friend Stinky. He seems like a nice boy."

"He is," I agreed. "He's a really cool guy."

"I'd like to meet his brother, too."

"Yeah," I said. "Hubble was a great guy, too."

"Your sister sure seemed to think so."

I gave a halfhearted gag. "Nita probably thought they were going to get married one day."

"Maybe they would have."

I thought about that. "I don't know. Maybe. It's hard for me to remember how Nita used to be. When Hubble went on the *Spirit* mission, and then disappeared . . . she got so mean and mad all the time. And I just pretended like Hubble never existed. I was afraid if I talked about Hubble, Stinky wouldn't want to be my friend anymore. Anyway . . ." I trailed off.

Larc patted my shoulder. "It must have been a real smack in the head to have everyone turn against you— even your sister."

"Smack in the face, you mean?" I started chewing my fingernails. "Yeah, it was. I mean, it's not like I had a million friends to start with, but yeah, I guess. Nita and I used to be friends. I just got lucky that Stinky didn't start hating me."

"Why would he have?" Larc asked softly.

"I . . . I should probably get going," I said abruptly, moving away from Larc. "It's getting late. I have to find out if I can get the com-bracelet hack to work, and if Mom and Dad have heard anything from Nita."

"Right," Larc said, putting her hands in her pockets. "Keep me updated."

I turned around to make my way out the door and spotted a framed certificate on the wall.

*Excellence in Teaching*

I made a face. Excellence in teaching, my butt. I reached up to wipe some dust off the glass so I could see the date on the certificate, and—*whoosh*—the door flew open.

Mrs. Halebopp stood there, with her black eyes wide as ever. It was the first time I'd ever seen her look startled. I immediately yanked my hand off the framed certificate. It was one of those instinctual yanks that you do when you're caught, and I totally pulled the frame off the wall by accident. It crashed to the floor and the glass shattered.

Mrs. Halebopp's startled look quickly turned into a scowl.

"S-sorry," I stammered. "I can clean it up." I knelt down and fumbled with some of the large pieces of glass.

"Leave it," she said in a hushed tone that meant she was already planning the recipe for boiling my hide.

"What's happening here, Larc?" she asked crisply, setting the book she was carrying onto a shelf and marching over to where Larc was standing. Mrs. H stood there, arms crossed, shooting fire from her eyes, and Larc, bless her amazing soul, launched into this long story about coming here to study because it was neutral territory, blah blah.

I was still kneeling by the broken glass when I saw a piece of paper that had slipped out from under the certificate. I couldn't see all of it, just the top part. It looked like a poem or something. I have no idea why I did it, but I snatched the piece of paper and shoved it deep into my pocket. I stood up. Larc and Mrs. H were still having a somewhat heated conversation about "boundaries" and "responsibilities" when I bolted out the door. Fight-or-flight had kicked in late. Thankfully, flight won.

After running at top speed for a few minutes, I stopped to catch my breath. The regulated seventy-two-degree temperature in the ship was suddenly feeling very hot. I didn't think Mrs. H was going to chase me, but I had run just to be sure. Now I was huffing and puffing, my mind struggling to make sense of what had happened. Why had I just opened up like that to Larc? I guess because she was nice. Crazy. But nice. And she seemed to like me, or at least like talking to me. And it had been so long since I'd had a friend other than Stinky.

I wiped my face and reached into my pocket.

"anyone lived in a pretty how town" by e. e. cummings.

Weird.

**It had been** almost a week since we'd found out about Nita. There was still no word from her. My secret attempt to hack Nita's com-bracelet was moving at a teeth-gnashingly slow pace. After the first success of hacking into Larc's monitor, I'd had no luck with anything. I was down to three hours of sleep a night, trying to get the stupid thing to work.

Understandably, Mom and Dad were even more preoccupied than usual. They spent almost all their free time locked in their bedroom. I tried listening through the door several times, but I could never hear anything.

They hardly noticed my sunken zombie eyes and I pretended not to care that they ignored me most of the time. None of us had mentioned anything about the whole "whoops, look who's on the computer monitor" thing, so it looked like that little catastrophe was going to pass under the radar. Whew.

I was now on my way to "rendezvous" with Stinky. My parents didn't know I was gone, and I had about twenty minutes until they woke up. Before calling Stink, though, I had something important to do. I'd tried to hack into the navigation system so that I could find out where the ship was going, but the code was taking me forever to penetrate. I'd tried asking Mom, but she just kept vaguely assuring me that everything was okay. She wouldn't say what the deal was with the plasma propulsion and I knew there was no way we could make it to Mars without a full charge. So if we weren't going to Mars, then where *were* we going? With Mom's suspicious answers I figured it'd just be faster to bust into the flight deck, take a quick look around, and figure it all out for myself. I had done some research (well, hacking) into the mainframe of the *Sojourner* and found the captain's personal and professional schedule. He was supposed to be in the gym having a morning workout. That meant the autopilot systems were running the ship and I could slip onto the flight deck without being spotted.

I walked quickly to the flight deck door at the front of the ship. Glancing around, I didn't see anyone, which was a miracle. I took a deep breath and stared at the keypad next to the locked door. It had one row of letters, one row of numbers, and one row of symbols. Dang.

I knew there was going to be a keypad, but I thought it was going to be a regular one, not a fancy-shmancy one. Dang. Dang. Double dang. My plan had been to try Mom's code for the house back on Earth.

Dang.

I looked over my shoulder again; then I held my breath and tried Mom's code anyway, just ignoring the letters and symbols. I was rewarded with the loudest buzz I'd ever heard. I winced and ducked, looking around for anyone who might have heard the deafening noise.

*One more try,* I thought, *and then I'm going to have to just take the time to hack the navigation system.* I steeled myself and steadied my finger.

I tried a trick Hubble had taught me. Most security systems have a backdoor code for emergency personnel and repairmen and people like that. The backdoor code for the keypad at home was every single key on the keypad, in order, one after the other. I gave it a whirl.

*Bzzzzzzzzzzz.*

I should have known that wouldn't work. . . . Too simple. I looked at my watch. Five minutes until I was supposed to contact Stinky. I was just going to give up, but I caught a flash of movement out of the corner of my eye.

Sugar Bear.

He was coming down the stairs from the observation deck and he was headed straight for me. It didn't look like he could see me—there was a tree kind of obscuring me—but he was heading down the stairs at a pants-on-fire pace. Had he heard the buzzes?

*Wait!* I suddenly remembered the keypad on our drivedropper at home. We hardly ever used it because Mom and Dad had remotes on their key chains, but it had the letters/numbers/symbols interface. I wasn't sure if I had it right or not, but I held my breath and tried the drivedropper code anyway. To my surprise, the keypad turned green. *Mom's really got to work on her security protocols,* I thought, laughing. The door whooshed open and I darted inside, just missing Shugabert.

Once on the flight deck, I took a minute to catch my breath. It would so suck if I had a heart attack.

"Mom?" I said, knowing she wasn't there. "Mom, are you here?" I figured it was a good cover if someone *was* here. I was just looking for my mom, right?

I glanced around the room. In a corner was the air lock capsule they used for spacewalking. The suits hung in the capsule, their huge helmets hanging limply, like decapitated ghosts. I shivered and walked over to a strange desk at the front of the room. It was placed in a clear alcove so that it looked like it was just floating in space. As I checked out all the computers and various equipment it held, one screen caught my attention. It had a red dot blipping along a curved line, kind of like a really old-fashioned radar screen. Under the blip, a list of coordinates streamed. From what I could tell, they were charting a path. Each coordinate had a corresponding date and time and—suddenly there was a loud . . .

*Whoooooooossssshhhhhh* . . .

I jumped about eighty-five feet into the air. Through the huge window, I saw feet gliding to a stop right above the now open outer door of the air lock capsule.

There was someone outside, and he was coming in!

I should have run right then, but I couldn't move. My breath was coming in short bursts and the room spun around me. I grabbed the table for support and watched as the feet floated into the air lock capsule.

*Aliens!* my brain screamed. *The ship is being taken over.*

Then there was another loud *whoooooooosh* and the floating figure in the capsule landed with a thunk on the floor. He had closed the hatch and flipped on the AutoGrav.

I watched in horror as he—the alien—whoever—removed his helmet.

Huh? It was the captain. And as soon as I recognized him, he saw me staring. I thought about running, but it was definitely too late for that.

"Son?" he said as the thick, clear plastic air lock door opened. "Michael Stellar? Is that you?"

Feeling all blood, sensation, and muscle control drain from my face, I tried to smile. "Oh, hi, Captain," I said in a strangled voice.

"What are you doing here?" he asked, his face clouding over. "This is a restricted area."

"I'm, uh, just looking for my mom," I answered, feeling proud that I remembered my cover story as I tried desperately to control my rising panic.

"She isn't at home getting ready for work?" he asked skeptically. I could see that he was looking me over, checking out my hands and the pockets of my jumpsuit.

"Uh. Maybe she is, actually," I said lamely. "I just, uh, didn't see her at breakfast, and, uh, Dad was in the shower, so I couldn't ask him, and so, uh, I thought I'd come looking for her." I was such a bad liar. I could feel my face burning.

"You best get home now, son. Your mom isn't due here for another hour. If she's not at your apartment, and your dad doesn't know where she is . . . well . . . come back and I'll call up a rescue party." He looked pretty stern still, but there was a small twinkle in his eye.

"Yes, sir," I answered, practically running for the door.

"Oh, and, Mike?"

"Yes?"

"Let's not mention this to anyone, okay? Some people frown on the captain of the ship flying around *outside* the ship."

I nodded and hightailed it out the door.

Right on cue my peapod buzzed. Stinky was going to love this.

19

I scooted into the men's room, climbed onto the toilet in the last stall, and took my usual position sitting on the tank.

Stinky kept saying, "Mike? Are you there?"

"Right here," I said quietly. "I was out in the hall, sorry."

"You sound . . . weird. Are you okay?"

"Man, Stinky, I just busted into the flight deck and—"

"You did *what*?"

"I busted into the flight deck. It was the only way to find out where the ship is going without waiting a billion years to hack into the system."

"Why couldn't you just ask your mom?" Stinky asked.

"Duh, knucklebutt, all ship movement is classified."

"Hey, don't call me knucklebutt, snotmunch."

"Sorry. It's been a very stressful morning."

"So what'd you find out?"

"The ship is definitely moving, and it's definitely still moving in the direction of the Fold. We're supposed to be there in three days."

"Whoa, that's fast!"

"I know. It doesn't make sense. Without time to power the plasma propulsion—"

"You'll never get—"

"To the other side of the Fold. I know."

We were both silent for a minute. And then Stinky started talking about not finding much in Mrs. H's old hard drives.

He laughed ruefully. "I don't know why I ever listen to you. 'You can get a detention so you can snoop in Mrs. H's things and blahdy blah blah,' " he said, imitating me in this annoying high-pitched voice. "Who knew throwing a flashnobang onstage during an assembly would cause *so* much trouble?"

I couldn't help laughing. "Oh, come on. I never told you to go crazy and momentarily blind the entire student population! I just meant toss one in homeroom and get an *afternoon* of detention or something. Not days and days and days."

"You suck." Stinky pouted for a moment. "Did you find anything else out while you were lurking around the ship? Mrs. H's true identity as a child-eating zombie?"

"Actually," I said, "I was in her apartment for a little bit last week."

I could tell that Stinky was stunned. "You broke into her apartment? Dude, I am *impressed*!"

"I didn't break in," I said, feeling my chest puff out with pride anyway. "But I did find something cool."

"What?"

"An old poem or something, written on actual paper. It fell out of a framed thing I accidentally broke."

"What's cool about that?"

"Don't know. But it was weird. Why would there be a poem hidden behind some dumb certificate in a frame?"

"Did you get caught?"

"I'm hurt, Stinky. Why would you automatically think I would get caught?"

"Because I know you, Mike. You think you're a good snoop, but you're not. So did you?"

"Yes," I said quietly.

Stinky let out a howl. "I guess you've been in detention for a week, too?"

"No," I said. "That's the really weird part. When she opened the door and saw me standing there, I just bolted. And she hasn't said anything to me about it. Larc must have said something to her."

"Larc?"

"Yeah. She was with me."

"You were in Mrs. H's apartment . . . alone with a girl? Dude, I am even *more* impressed!"

I felt myself blush. "It was nothing like that. We were running away from someone and she had a key to Mrs. H's apartment."

"Who were you running away from?" Stinky asked excitedly. "Man, you move to outer space for a week and suddenly you've turned into Space Agent Stellar!"

My blush deepened. "It's a long story, and I kinda have to go now, Stink. I really, really, *really* need to get home before my parents wake up."

"Okay—but you owe me a story."

"Hey, Stink?"

"Yeah?"

"Once I'm out near the Fold, these peapods are just going to be shiny little balls of metal."

"I know, man." Stinky paused. "Hey. Have you heard anything about Neeters?"

"I'm working on a hack for her com-bracelet, so hopefully in the next day or so I'll try to contact her."

"Well, give me a buzz if you find anything out, okay? If I don't hear from you, I'll just figure your sad little brain couldn't handle the onslaught of work it's having to do these days."

"Ha-ha, frog lips." Now it was my turn to pause. "If

we do go out of range before you and I talk again, Stink, well, thanks for being there to help me out with all of this crazy stuff. You really are a great friend." I hadn't expected to say the long good-bye to Stinky this morning and I felt a little awkward.

"Yeah, yeah, fartblossom, you're a good friend, too."

We both laughed.

"See you, man," I said.

"See you."

I put the peapod back in my pocket and headed out of the restroom toward the apartment. I needed to hustle.

**I snuck through** the front door and hurried to my room, trying not to alert any of Mr. Shugabert's motion-activated messages.

Once in my room, I pushed the square button on the far wall, and my desk and computer slid up from the floor. A bench popped out under the desk and I sat down and powered up my computer. I synced up my handheld to the computer so I could get a readout of the progress on my com-bracelet hack.

Looking down at my handheld, I caught a flash of light out of the corner of my eye. I glanced up and saw a small IM pictoscreen in the corner of my monitor. Weird. The image was fuzzy and black and white, which was even stranger. Squinting, I leaned closer to the monitor to see what was going on.

I gasped.

It was Nita! My hack had worked!

"Mike?" Nita's voice was barely audible over the static. "Is that you?"

"Nita?" I said into the built-in microphone on my computer.

"I don't . . . lot of time, Mi . . ." She was breaking up badly. But I could tell there was something in her voice. Something I didn't recognize. She was . . . scared.

"Your com-bracelet," I blurted. "The hack . . . it worked. . . . I should go get Mom and Dad." I stood up quickly, tripping on the bench.

"No." She propelled her face closer to the bracelet. "Not get . . . and Dad. Just shut up and li . . . to me."

Ah. There was the Nita I recognized. Here I was the one who found *her* and she was giving the orders.

She continued at a fast clip with only a few words clear enough for me to hear. "I need . . . tell you some important . . . Mike. And I don't want . . . ask any . . . or do anything stupid."

"Nita. Wait. I can't understand you. Let me mess with the signal for a minute. . . . Can you just keep talking so I can—"

"I just said . . . Mike. Just shut . . . and lis—"

"Where are you?" I interrupted. "Are you okay? Are you with the EFEs?"

She nodded. "Long story . . ."

"So *you* did this," I said, surprised at the anger welling up in me. "You ran off on purpose?"

She shook her head. "Not now . . . No time. I've uncovered . . . information, Mike . . . last Mars mission . . ."

She was barely coming through at all now and I impulsively smacked my computer monitor to try to miraculously fix the poor reception.

". . . passenger manifest . . . last trip . . . Hazelwood . . ."

There was a pause, and I thought the connection had been broken. I jumped up and nearly turned the computer off so that I could try to manually boost the signal. But her image appeared again. I stared at the salt-and-pepper static of her face and scrunched up my own. Her mouth was moving again, but I couldn't hear anything. I kept motioning with my arms and cupping my hands to my ears to indicate to her that I couldn't hear her. Then I felt like a moron. Just because I couldn't hear her, it didn't mean she couldn't hear me.

I leaned in close to the microphone and said, "I can't hear anything you're sa—"

Suddenly her voice crackled back to life. She sounded impatient. "Da . . . Hazelwood . . . *president* . . . Project!"

"*David* Hazelwood?" I asked. Was Nita saying that David Hazelwood had been on the first mission? She couldn't be. That wouldn't make any sense at all. The company would never have risked sending their then president out on a dangerous mission. Besides, after two years the public would have heard about his disappearance. Mom said he had "retired early."

Nita's mouth was again moving with no sound. Finally her voice rang out: "*Sabotaged* the ship!"

It took a second for what she had said to sink in and then I was flabbergasted.

"What? Who sabotaged the ship? David Hazelwood? Which ship?" I felt my stomach turn ice-cold. "Nita? What are you talking about?"

". . . ora. Mike . . . she knows. No-bid contracts . . . destruction . . . all planets . . . terraform. Destroy."

She wasn't making any sense at all now. I grabbed my handheld and started writing down the words she was saying. Maybe I could puzzle them together.

Nita was still talking, faster now and in a lower voice. "Haze . . . company charter. Aurora . . . money-crazed. *Spirit* . . . lost . . . Fold. Hub . . . will know. Must find . . . Suspicious . . . Mom and Da—"

I was scribbling like crazy, trying to take down every sound she was making.

". . . isn't safe. EFEs . . . they say . . . Hubble . . . alive."

"Nita!" I nearly shouted. "Slow down. I can't understand y—" But she was barreling on.

"Can't tell . . . Mom and Dad. . . . Think . . . danger.

You, too. *Sojourner* is going to be . . . just like . . . *Spirit* was . . . Aurora. Cover-up. Not a secret."

My mind was spinning. This was amazing! Someone other than me or Stinky had finally mentioned something about a cover-up.

"Nita . . . ," I pleaded, "I can't understand what you're saying. What do you mean 'cover-up'? Can you say that last part over again?"

And then the only full sentence to come through during the entire "conversation" screeched out of the computer, crystal-clear.

"Mom and Dad are *in on the sabotage.*"

**That took the** breath right out of me. I sat there spluttering, not able to form words. She abruptly stopped talking and turned her head. I heard muffled shouting and saw the room fly around as Nita's arms waved like they do when she gets really mad. I heard a distinct hair ball noise and then the screen went blank.

"Nita?" I nearly yelled into the microphone. *"Nita?"* She was gone.

I sat back in my chair, my brain swimming. Sabotage? Mom and Dad? David Hazelwood on the *Spirit*?

From the hallway, Mom's voice interrupted my racing thoughts. "Is everything all right in there, Mike? Were you just shouting something?"

I opened my door. "Just, uh, practicing my report, Mom."

Mom talked over her shoulder as she walked to the kitchen. "Shouting is not proper form for public speaking, Mike. Now, come eat your breakfast and then we can call Gram and see if she's found anything out about Nita."

I felt my stomach knot up. With the *Sojourner* getting closer to the Fold, I wouldn't be able to contact Nita anymore, even with the greatest hacking skills in the universe. And the peapod would be useless soon, so Stinky couldn't help, either. If I was going to figure out what Nita was trying to tell me, I had to do it quickly. And if Mom and Dad were sabotaging this mission, or had sabotaged the last one . . . well, I was going to have to figure out what was going on without their help.

I was anxious the whole time we were in the Family Room. Mom talked to Gram for only a few minutes, but I felt my face flushing the entire time. I knew I should tell them that I'd found Nita, but she had said so many unsettling things. I just wanted to sit down with my handheld and look at my scribbles.

"Right, Mike?" Mom was looking at me expectantly.

"Huh?"

"It's okay if Dad walks you to class, right?"

"What? Why?"

Dad didn't say anything. He just opened the door to the Family Room and motioned for me to go out first.

I stood up from the couch and said, "So that's it? Gram had no news?"

Mom sighed. "I just *told* you, Mike. The task force is still investigating."

"Come on, kiddo," Dad said, his expression softening. "Let's get you to class."

Mom grabbed me in a hug and I guiltily hugged her back. Then I picked up my bag and headed out the door with Dad right behind me. We walked to my classroom in silence. I needed to talk to Stinky about Nita . . . but it didn't look like I was going to get that chance. I'd tried the going-to-the-bathroom thing too many times lately and Mrs. Halebopp was only letting me go during lunchtime now. She knew I was up to something. I was pretty sure she could somehow read my mind.

And then there was my report. With all of the other researching and hacking I'd been doing, I'd practically forgotten all about it. Now it was due at the end of the week and I was going to have to really hustle. Not only that, but the detention from ages ago that I'd never served was happening after class today.

"Have a good day, Mike," Dad said. We were standing in front of the classroom door. It was open. Larc was inside staring at me.

The area around us darkened from the tower of Mrs. Halebopp's hair blocking out the artificial light. She cleared her throat. "Mr. Stellar?"

Dad shook her outstretched claw.

"Has Michael informed you of his detention this afternoon? I'm afraid he may be late for dinner this evening."

"Detention?" Dad asked, looking at me, his smile fading.

"It's an old one," I muttered. "Remember? From last week. Larc'll be there, too."

"I'll see that young Mr. Stellar learns the value of good behavior if it takes a detention every evening," Mrs. Halebopp said, mostly to herself, though her face was aimed at Dad's.

Dad frowned. "Behave yourself today, okay?"

I sighed and walked into the classroom. As I took my seat, I saw Dad's and Mrs. Halebopp's heads bowed together. They were talking, and I didn't like it.

Larc turned around in her seat and gave me a thoughtful look. "You look like a three-day-old burrito," she said.

I made a face. "What does that even *mean*?"

"You look bad. Tired. Sad."

"Well, much like a three-day-old burrito," I said, riffing on her weird analogy, "I have noticed that things around here stink."

"Well, it's not me," Larc said, shaking her head and trying to get a whiff of her hair.

I laughed. "No, I mean figuratively. Something fishy is going on."

I tried to think of the best way to tell her what had happened this morning. I didn't want to blurt it out in the middle of class. Mrs. H probably had bugs under all our desks. I decided to wait until detention. Mrs. H was pretty reliable about handing out manual-labor punishments. So if Larc and I had to swab the decks or e-file some papers, we might be able to quietly talk.

I leaned forward in my desk and carefully tapped Larc on the shoulder. "Do you think we can talk during detention?"

"Michael Stellar, are you asking me to the *Sojourner* Space Prom?" She turned and batted her icy eyes at me.

"What?" I spluttered. "There's no . . . What in the world are you talking about?"

Mrs. Halebopp cleared her throat and looked at us menacingly. I sat back in my chair and Larc leaned forward in hers. Mrs. H walked to the front of the room to begin the day's lesson. I could hardly concentrate on what she was saying. I just tapped my foot and waited for detention.

## 22

"**Against my better** judgment I'm letting you two serve your detentions together this afternoon."

Mrs. Halebopp had her hands clasped behind her back and she was pacing. She shot us both a grimace. Her hair was teetering forward even more than usual and it looked like it was leading her down the aisle as she marched back and forth.

"I don't want to hear any talking, see any smirks, or catch even a glimpse of either one of you turning around in your seats. You are to research your reports in silence. Communication is forbidden."

I sighed. Great. No sweeping or filing. How were Larc and I supposed to talk?

Mrs. H continued. "I've turned on the wireless port. You should be able to access the Universal Network through the mainframe on the ship. There you'll be granted access to the library's reference section and you can work on your reports. Your password is your birthday. Now, Larc, honey, I want you to come sit over here."

She motioned for Larc to take a seat at the other end of the classroom with her back facing me.

"Michael. You stay where you are."

I nodded, feeling the world drop away. There was no way Larc and I could even *try* to talk now. Mrs. H unclasped her hands and smoothed her hair as she walked back to her desk. She swayed a little and it looked like she was collapsing under the weight of her hairdo. I snickered and she wheeled around like I'd jabbed her with a curlzapper.

"What was that, Mr. Stellar?"

"Oh, uh, nothing," I mumbled, "just a, you know, tickle in my throat."

"Well, I suggest you resolve your tickles right now. There is to be silence in this room." She took her seat behind her desk and glared at me. I picked up my handheld and initiated my link with the mainframe. Then I had a brain wave. I tapped a couple of commands into the handheld and waited for a second.

"Link Failure."

*Dang,* I thought. I tapped the screen and tried again.

"Link Failure."

Come *on. . . .*

I tapped out a few more commands and waited. I glanced over at Larc. I couldn't figure out what she was doing. She was just sitting there. The only sound in the room was my tapping.

Finally a box popped up on my handheld screen.

"Act normal," I typed.

"Took you long enough," she wrote back. I smiled.

"I hacked the wireless port to connect our handhelds," I wrote.

"Duh," Larc wrote back.

"Take a look at these notes," I tapped out as I quickly uploaded my scribbles to Larc's handheld. "I talked to Nita this morning. Our connection was terrible. The things she said . . . Bad." I hit Send and waited.

Larc took forever. With only ten minutes of detention left, I sent her a note to see if she had come up with any ideas. No response. I sent another note. Still no response. Then, finally, the familiar little white box popped onto the screen.

"This is not good."

"What is not good?" I wrote back right away.

"David Hazelwood on the ship. Money-crazed Aurora. Sabotage. Your parents. Mike, this is bad."

My shoulders slumped. I already knew it was bad. I was hoping Larc would see something different.

"It looks like my parents really did sabotage the first trip, doesn't it?" I wrote as my stomach filled with lead.

"I thought she was talking about them sabotaging *this* trip."

I sighed. Larc was confirming all my fears.

"I told you. Bad," she wrote.

I just had such a hard time believing Mom and Dad were the bad guys. Yet Nita's crackly voice kept running through my head.

Another message from Larc broke my concentration: "Are you OK?"

"Fine," I typed back. "I'm just trying to figure out my next step."

Knowing Larc, I expected to see a suggestion for my next step right away, but there was nothing.

I glanced up at Mrs. H. She was reading a book. I couldn't quite make out its title, but the cover was a gaudy orange and red. It was funny to see her with an actual book in her hands. The only other person I knew who read old books anymore was Dad.

And then I saw it.

The title of the book, its gold lettering flashing in the fluorescent lighting, was *anthology: the life works of e. e. cummings*.

Suddenly Mrs. H looked up and caught me gawking. For a few seconds our eyes locked. I could hardly believe it, but she almost seemed to *smile* at me. A moment later there was a buzz and the classroom intercom said, "Beatrice Halebopp, the ship administrator would like a quick word." She closed her book with a *thwap* and set it on her desk.

Grumbling, she stood up. "Please stay in your seats. Do not move. Do not talk. Continue studying. I'll be back in five minutes. And if you think I can't see you while I'm gone, then you're more naive than I thought." With that, she walked briskly from the room. The door whooshed shut behind her and Larc and I were alone.

**We sat there** stunned for a few seconds before I whispered, "Go stand by the door, will you?"

Larc's eyes widened. "She just said she could see us, Mike!" she whispered fiercely.

"I'm calling her bluff," I said. "Go stand by the door. Give me a whistle when you see her coming." I jumped up and ran to Mrs. H's desk. Larc hustled to stand by the door.

"How am I supposed to see anything? Door's shut, brainiac."

I ran and hit the button to open the door. It flew up and startled me. I still wasn't used to doors that flew up instead of out. I dropped the stylus to my handheld in the doorway and whacked the button, closing the door. This left a tiny gap for Larc to peer through.

"Now get on your belly," I ordered. "When you see those awful shoes clicking toward you, give me a signal."

Larc looked annoyed at my bossiness, but she did what I asked. I ran back to the desk and grabbed the book. Frantically flipping through the pages, I felt my heart leap when I looked at the page numbers. The book started on page 212. Why would she have ripped out all those pages? I yanked the page from the frame out of my pocket. It had page number 259 on one side and 260 on the other. I flipped through Mrs. H's book; 259 wasn't missing. It was right there in the book. I flattened the page from my pocket onto Mrs. H's desk and compared it to the page in the book. They were exactly alike. No changes that I could see at all.

Weird. Weird. Weird.

I flipped through the rest of the pages, but they all looked normal, too.

My heart stopped. Larc was waving her hand at me and chirping this strangled *cuckoo cuckoo* noise. I quickly flipped to the first page of the book, ripped it out, and stuffed it into my pocket. Larc was up on her feet and scrambling to her desk. We brushed by each other.

"Cuckoo?" I whispered.

"I don't know how the heck to whistle," she said.

I landed in my seat with an *oof* just as Mrs. H opened the door and walked back into the room.

I struggled to keep my breathing normal, even

though my heart was leaping out of my chest. Mrs. H looked at me accusingly, but she didn't say anything.

After just enough time to catch my breath, the teetering beehive shook as Mrs. H stood. "Detention is over. Thank you for your good behavior this evening. It was a pleasant surprise. Now, go home, both of you. And I don't want to see you in another detention again."

Larc and I stood quickly, murmured our good-byes to Mrs. H, and bolted out of the room.

Once we were in the hall and out of earshot, Larc gasped, "You are a crazy man!"

I nodded and laughed. "Hey, I had to seize the moment."

"Whatever," was Larc's retort. "I've never once been in trouble with my aunt—until I met you, Michael Stellar."

"Well, you're not in trouble anymore, are you? We didn't get caught, did we?"

"*You* didn't get caught," she said. "Why is that book so important, anyway?"

I stood there, not understanding why Larc wasn't understanding. Then it dawned on me. I'd never told her about the page from the broken frame. I frantically reached into my pocket and pulled out the rumpled sheet of paper.

"This was hidden in the frame I broke back at Mrs. Halebopp's apartment," I said breathlessly.

Larc looked at the paper skeptically. "It's just a poem."

"From a book just like the one on her desk!" I said excitedly.

Larc looked at me curiously. "I still don't get it."

"Why was it hidden?" I nearly shouted. "And why is she reading a *real* book and not using readers?" My mind was racing. . . . There had to be something to this. There just *had* to be.

"I don't know, Mike," Larc said cautiously. "Aunt Beebo likes poetry, especially twentieth-century stuff like this one. She has a lot of old poetry books. She says she likes the way the pages feel between her fingers."

"But why was this hidden in the frame?" I asked, waving the paper in Larc's face. "Why would a ripped-out page from a book be hidden behind an old certificate?"

"I don't know, Mike," Larc said impatiently. "Don't you think we have enough mysteries to solve right now?"

"But, Larc," I interrupted, wanting desperately for her to feel the excitement that was welling up inside me, "almost all of the pages of her book were ripped out. Don't you want to figure out why?"

Larc looked at me long and hard. Finally she sighed. "Okay. I believe you. There's something bizarre about that book. But, Mike, we can't worry about some old book right now. Have you already forgotten about your par—"

"Of course not," I snapped, angrily stuffing the page back into my pocket. "I just think there's something to this."

"You have to talk to your parents," Larc said. "You can't just hide from that, Mike."

I shook my head. "No. I can't talk to them. Not now. Not if they're planning to sabotage the ship." I felt the energy drain from my system. "I mean, if that's what they're really doing, Larc, then *they're* the bad guys." Things were becoming disturbingly clear as I said them out loud. "This whole time, I've been angry at everyone for believing that my parents were in on some conspiracy. But, Larc, it seems like Nita was trying to tell me that they really *are* the bad guys. They *have* been covering things up."

It all started to make sense. Why my parents had been acting so weird . . . why they were so distracted . . . even why Mr. Shugabert was watching the family so closely. My eyes widened as the thought occurred to me. The Project must suspect them of something, and that was why Mr. Shugabert seemed to be everywhere. He wasn't on the trip just to be Mom's executive assistant and regular ol' Stellar Family Pain in the Bootie. He was there keeping an eye on everything. He *knew* they were up to something.

"Sugar Bear," I whispered to myself, "he's a *good-guy* spy?"

"Huh? Did you say something?" Larc had wandered over to look out one of the windows in the lobby.

"No, I just . . ." I trailed off, seeing the window behind Larc. "Whoa. Is that the . . . ?"

Larc nodded solemnly. "It's the Fold. We're coming up on it fast now. I bet we launch tomorrow. Maybe even tonight."

Out the window was a seething black mass. It looked like heat waves over hot pavement—nearly invisible, but clearly there, writhing, furious. Every now and then sparks of color would shoot around its perimeter, giving us a better idea of its size and shape. It was kind of like a big doorway. But it was in constant motion, growing wider one minute and taller the next, then back down to the size it was before.

"It looks like it's alive," I said in a near whisper. "It looks like it's *breathing*."

Larc and I walked closer to the window. I felt her take my hand and I wasn't embarrassed at all. That seething mass made me feel small and insignificant. It wasn't a feeling I liked.

"You know how a bee must feel as it's hurtling toward the windshield of an electri-bus?" I asked Larc quietly. "That thing gives me the same feeling."

After staring at the Fold and watching it move closer to us, Larc and I both wanted to move farther away from it. We wandered down the halls of the ship, looking for a quiet place to sit and talk. I knew I'd be in crazy trouble for being late to dinner, but I didn't care. Right now having Mom and Dad mad at me for not eating my soy patties on time seemed ridiculous. We stopped outside the library. There was a bench to sit on and no one around. So we sat. We were still holding hands, though now it did feel a little awkward, and I took my hand back. It was all sweaty and hot—almost burning. I wiped it on the inside of my pocket.

"Where were we?" Larc asked quietly, looking up at me intently.

"Uh," I said, feeling a blush come to my cheeks, "I think we were talking about my parents being traitors."

"Oh, right." She looked away.

"And I said that I thought Sugar Bear might be a good-guy spy," I offered.

"You did?"

"Just before we saw the Fold."

"Oh."

"So now what? My parents are planning on destroying this mission just like the last one. Or so it seems. I guess the first thing we should do is try to stop them."

"But think about it, Mike. Why would they want to destroy the *Sojourner*? They're *on* the ship."

"I *have* been thinking about it, Larc. It's *all* I can think about. I mean, maybe that glowing escape pod that Dad didn't want me to find out about has something to do with their evil plan. Even Sugar Bear was checking it out the other day."

"I still think you should ask them about your suspicions," Larc said. "Before you do anything crazy."

"No way. They'll just lie to me. They've been lying to me this whole time. For two years!" I stood up and paced in front of the bench. "I just can't believe it, Larc." I put my face in my hands and mumbled, "This is so much harder than researching a speech. I should have just researched my speech and not messed with any of this crazy stuff."

Larc touched my elbow, pulling me back down to the bench.

"Don't say that, Mike. I mean, yes, studying is important. But so is this. You should know who your parents are and what they're up to." She paused. "I never knew mine."

"What do you mean? What about your dad?"

"He's not really my dad."

"He's not?" I looked at Larc, shocked. "But he's so tall."

She pinched me. "All tall people aren't related, Mike."

"If he's not your dad, then who . . ."

"He's my—"

"Well, well, well . . ." Mr. Shugabert walked around the corner and nearly gave me a stroke. He must have specially padded shoes; why couldn't I ever hear him coming?

"What have we here?" Shugabert shot us his million-watt grin. "Two little lovebirds making a nest?"

We didn't say anything. Larc scooched closer to me on the bench, though.

"Isn't it late for two youngsters to be out roaming the halls?" he asked. I could tell he was trying to seem cool and friendly, but there was something about his eyes. They narrowed ever so slightly.

"What are you kids up to, anyway? I made some excellent soy patties for supper, Mike. I even made enough for Larc. Of course, they're probably cold by now. . . ."

"We're not hungry," I muttered.

"Oh, is that right?" He tried to laugh and it came out sounding like a strangled cough.

"You know, technically, it isn't in my job description to cook dinner for Marie or her family. In fact, I'm late to a meeting because I stayed to whip up some food for you guys. But since Marie is so busy, I thought it would be nice to help her out with dinner."

"What kind of meeting?" I asked.

The question seemed to catch him off guard. "Oh . . . you know. With all the other executive assistants."

"That's funny," Larc piped up. "I haven't really seen a lot of other executive assistants, have you, Mike?"

"Uh-uh," I said. "Just think of what everyone is missing, not having the disembodied voice of a dude acting as their alarm clock. No cold soy patties waiting for them when they get home after a hard day of work . . ."

Mr. Shugabert could tell we were testing him, and a vein in his neck started to throb as his smile grew bigger and bigger until it threatened to eat his face.

"Come to mention it," I said, "you do a lot of helping out with family stuff, don't you? You're kind of, uh, always around, aren't you?"

"It must be exhausting," Larc said, shaking her head.

"Just doing my job," he said. The vein in his neck was keeping its own little high-speed techno beat.

"Listen," I said, "I'm going through a . . . *thing* right now and I just want to sit here with my friend and talk for a little while. I promise I'll be home soon."

Mr. Shugabert began to pace in front of me and Larc like a panther ready to pounce. But I was the one who pounced. Something in me snapped.

"What are you up to?" I asked suddenly, my eyes flashing. "We're just quietly sitting here, minding our own business, and you appear. Whenever I walk down a hallway, you're there. Whenever I do *anything*, you're there. What is *up* with that? You're not *my* executive assistant. You're just my . . . Sugar Bear."

"Mi-ike," Larc said out of the corner of her mouth. "That was a *terrible* rhyme." And then she laughed like she was being tickled from the inside out.

Sugar Bear lost it. "Stop calling me that!" he said angrily.

"You're just a big, stupid . . . *spy*," I said.

Larc's eyes widened so much I thought they might pop out of her head. Mr. Shugabert lunged toward me. *This is not how I want to die.*

He grabbed my arm. "If it wasn't for Aurora telling me to keep my hands off, you'd be toast right now, little boy. I'd have locked you in a closet days ago!"

He gave me a good shake and I seized the moment. I slipped my loose hand into his jacket pocket. My fingers tightened around his handheld. As he gave me another rough shake, I yanked my hand out of his pocket and shoved it into mine. He suddenly let me go and I bounced roughly back against the bench.

"Look at me, tiny man," Mr. Shugabert said, seething. He grabbed my face and squeezed my cheeks together. "Aurora didn't say anything about me keeping my hands off your parents. You better tell them to watch out. Aurora's not stupid. She knows what they're—" He abruptly stopped talking, as if he realized he was saying too much. He let go of my face and walked away without another word.

"You think he just resigned?" I asked Larc, clutching my chest and hoping I wasn't having a heart attack.

"I have no idea." Larc looked at me with wonder.

I alternately rubbed my cheeks and my arm and said, "I guess taunting him on purpose wasn't such a swell idea." Larc's eyes widened. "But we know good guys don't threaten kids and toss them up against benches." I paused and rubbed my arm again. "Hey, look what I got besides a big bruise and a heart attack. . . ."

I yanked Mr. Shugabert's handheld from my pocket and grinned.

Larc's mouth fell open and her blue braces glinted. "Michael Stellar, you have quite the sticky digits!"

174

I felt my chest puff out. "Hey, I'm just trying to find out what's going on arou—"

"Mike, look. . . ." Larc cut me off and pointed out the window. The stars were streaking by. The ship had picked up considerable speed in just the past few minutes.

"We're going to be at the Fold practically any minute now," Larc said somberly, watching the stars fly by outside the window.

"I guess I have to talk to my parents," I said, stuffing the handheld in my pocket and mustering my courage.

"You have to, Mike. Just tell them what you know. They can't deny everything. Especially when you tell them you've heard from Nita."

I took a deep breath and said, "I know. I know."

"Find me before school tomorrow. Tell me everything you find out. I want to help, Mike. I—" She stopped talking and grabbed me in a slightly off-balance hug. I hugged her back and started feeling warm in places I didn't want to feel warm in.

I backed away and said, "Okay. I'll find you in the morning."

"Good luck, Mike."

"Thanks," I said, turning toward the hallway to my apartment. "And now that I know Sugar Bear isn't a good guy . . . well, by default that makes Mom and Dad good guys."

Maybe.

**25**

I looked at Mom rubbing her temple and quietly spooning a sloppy soy patty into her mouth. There was just no way she could be part of an evil conspiracy to sabotage this mission.

"Mike?" Mom looked up from her dinner. "You do realize you are completely and utterly grounded until we get to Mars, right?"

I swallowed. This was it.

"Hey." Dad walked up behind me and put his hand on my shoulder. "Your mom and I are incredibly anxious to hear why you're so late." The quietness in his voice scared me.

"Um," I mumbled. I gave furious thought to what I should say. "Mom . . . Dad . . . ," I began, gathering all my courage. "I have something to ask you—"

A voice crackled through Dad's handheld. "Mr. Stellar, you have an emergency patient at your office."

Dad stood up, dropping his napkin onto his plate and wiping his hands on the front of his jumpsuit instead. "Uh-oh. I wonder what that's all about." He started walking out of the room.

"But, Dad, wait. I need to—"

"I have to go, Mike," he said impatiently, looking suddenly more worried than angry. "There's an emergency. Here, I almost forgot." Dad reached into his pocket and handed me my evening vial of stomach-settling vitamin gunk.

"But it's important, Dad. . . . I—"

"Mrs. Stellar, you are wanted on the flight deck." This time it was Mom's handheld crackling to life.

"Great," said Mom, shooting Dad a look I couldn't figure out. "Mike, are you going to be okay by yourself? No sneaking around, no getting into trouble?" She gave me a threatening look.

"I'll be fine," I answered hastily, sensing that the time for me to ask my parents about the sabotage was quickly slipping away. But I had to talk to them *now*. With the ship moving so fast and the Fold coming up so quickly . . . If they really were sabotaging the ship like they sabotaged the *Spirit*, then it would all be happening when we entered the Fold. And that was only hours away.

"Please inform flight deck I'm on my way," Mom said into her handheld, and then stuffed it into her workbag.

Before I could say anything, Mom was out the door. Then Dad came rushing by in such a hurry that his medical bag banged against his leg.

He pointed threateningly at me and said, "Stay here. Don't move. We'll talk when Mom and I get back." Then he was out the door, too.

I just sat there at the kitchen table, blinking in astonishment. I was ready for a confrontation, and now I was all alone. Should I follow them? Just shout things at them down the hallway?

I dropped my head onto the table and groaned. We were all about to be lost in space—or vaporized—and I was the only one who could do anything to stop it. I jumped up, swallowing my fear of parental retribution, and decided to chase after them. On my way to the front door, though, I passed the door to Mom and Dad's bedroom. For the first time in days, the door was ajar and I could see in.

Forgetting about my plan to run screaming like a maniac down the halls of the ship, I crept to the bedroom doorway and peered into their room. I'd been trying for so long to hear what was going on in this room; it felt strange to see into it. I didn't know what

I'd expected, but it didn't look weird. Just . . . normal. Like on the first day we arrived on the ship.

Feeling stupid for creeping around when no one was in the apartment to catch me, I tried to prove to myself that I was brave by giving the bedroom door a kick and causing it to whoosh open all the way.

I stepped into their bedroom. All the furniture was tucked away, so it looked like an empty room right now. I couldn't help glancing over my shoulder as I walked farther into their room. Now that I knew that Mr. Shugabert really *had* been spying on us, I had this creepy, continual feeling of being watched. I punched a couple of buttons, and a chair and a small bookcase appeared.

I knelt by the bookcase. It didn't surprise me that it was full. Dad's box from home had been almost totally filled with books to bring on the move.

Running my finger down the spine of the first book, I felt . . . confused. I'd never bothered to actually read the book Mrs. H gave me for my research paper, but I could swear that this book on Dad's shelf was the exact same one she'd given to me. But why would Dad put it on his shelf? He knew I was going to have to give it back.

I had that puzzle-piece feeling again. Something was going on, but I couldn't quite . . . I ran my finger down the spines of all the books, reading their titles. My heartbeat quickened. Right there in front of me was *anthology: the life works of e. e. cummings*.

I gasped and looked at the next book, and the next one, and the next one. Every single book on Dad's shelf was an anthology of some twentieth-century poet—just like all the books had been in Mrs. H's apartment. I sat there, stunned.

I pulled the e. e. cummings book off the shelf and opened it. The first hundred pages or so had been ripped out, the same as with Mrs. Halebopp's! I pulled the wadded-up pages from my pocket and spread them out on the floor in front of me. First there was the one from the frame in Mrs. H's apartment and then there was the one I'd ripped out of the book while I was in detention.

As I felt excitement rise from my toes, I looked at the number of the first page in Dad's book: 261.

I did one of those exhale-laugh things and abandoned the awkward crouch I'd been in. I sat hard on the floor. How did a page from Dad's book get into a frame in Mrs. H's apartment? I started yanking books off the shelf and opening them.

Every single book was missing pages.

Every.

Single.

Book.

"What does this mean?" I kept whispering as I thumbed through the books. I couldn't see anything weird about them—other than that they were missing pages. I sat there, stumped.

It felt like I'd been sitting there for hours, my excitement turning to frustration. The ship would be reaching the Fold practically any minute now. Mom and Dad had disappeared—probably to begin the sabotage, I realized with a sick feeling. Evil Mrs. Halebopp was probably somehow involved, too, and I was stuck here in this stupid apartment, with these stupid books. There was nothing I could do about anything.

I helplessly fanned through the pages of one book after another, thinking of those antique flip-books where a little cartoon of a man or a dog dances a jig as you fly through the pages. There were no cartoons in any of these books. But I did notice something weird. As I flipped, I could feel the texture of the paper changing from page to page. I stopped flipping and ran my hand over the surface of a page.

The page felt . . . what was it? Bumpy? I couldn't see anything out of the ordinary, but I could definitely feel something strange. The bumps weren't everywhere, just here and there. I grabbed Mrs. H's pages off the floor and felt them. They had bumps, too!

Now things were getting interesting.

I ripped a page from one of the books and rubbed it

again and again, feeling the bumps and trying to figure out what the heck they were. It was as if someone had stabbed them with a straight pin, leaving eeny-weeny holes everywhere.

Suddenly my brain flashed on something Larc had said—about Mrs. H. "She says she likes the way the pages feel between her fingers." Larc's voice echoed in my head.

"It's a code!" I shouted into the empty room. "It has to be! Just like on *MonsterMetalMachines* #732 when Preditator is taken hostage by the Extermibus! Preditator used some old thing called Morse code," I muttered to myself. "Maybe that's what this is."

I sat for what felt like forever, staring at the bumps, feeling the bumps, rubbing the pages over my face, growling into my hands. . . . Finally I turned each of the three ripped-out pages over and stared at the poems.

*Maybe this is all a trick to get me to read more poetry.* I held the pages up one at a time and read them.

What the . . . ?

In my surprise, I jumped up. My white-hot intensity had worked! I'd just seen tiny little pinpricks of light shooting through the page. Almost imperceptible, under certain letters there was definitely a tiny pinprick. The light from the ambient lamp on the wall had shone through the holes when I'd held the page up.

"*Aha!*" I shouted crazily, and laughed out loud. I started trying to decipher the code.

I smacked a button on the wall and Mom's desk appeared. I grabbed the nearest household handheld and activated the voice-recognition application. I read out loud all the letters from Mrs. H's page that had a pinprick underneath them.

"ANEWMISSIONVENUSALDRINREACTIVATED UNDERCOVERTEACHERHALEBOPPHAVEINSTIGATED CONTACTWITHSPIRITNEEDHELPLOCATING SHIPTOPSECRET"

It took only a few minutes for me to figure out the words.

"A new mission. Venus Aldrin reactivated. Undercover teacher Halebopp. Have instigated contact with *Spirit*. Need help locating ship. Top-secret."

"Holy mother of donkeys," I gasped. "Mrs. Halebopp is Venus Aldrin."

**Venus Aldrin was** the most decorated search-and-rescue astronaut the Project had ever employed. We'd studied her in school. In fact, I'd probably just failed that pop quiz on her. She was supposed to be retired—living anonymously in a village somewhere in the desert.

I started opening all the books and feeling their pages. The first page of every book had pinpricks. Time stood still as I sat, decoding the messages.

One of them said something about the *Spirit* confirming David Hazelwood's presence. Another said, "Food dwindling, Aurora refuses to send S&R crew." Another had a bit that said, "Hubble Hawking confirmed alive."

*"Hubble's alive!"* I said.

Another message read, "NS deep cover planned. EFE infiltration to commence 6/1." I slapped myself on the forehead. *That* was why Nita hadn't come on the trip. She was undercover with the EFEs? Then why not just contact Mom and Dad and tell them what she'd found out?

The next book's message said, "Aurora hand in sabotage confirmed. Her transmission of virus succeeded. *Spirit* not repairable." I swallowed, wondering what the next book would tell me.

It said, "A&M chosen. J's assistance vital. V reached agreement with school, is on board. Operation Fight Back to commence."

So this confirmed it. "A&M" had to be Mom and Dad—Albert and Marie. "J" was probably Jim—Larc's dad. And "V" was Venus. The "agreement with school" part proved that Mrs. Halebopp really was Venus Aldrin.

I sat back, stunned. It was all starting to make sense. Venus Aldrin would *have* to be undercover; there was no way Aurora would have let her come back to the Project, if Aurora was preventing a search-and-rescue mission to the *Spirit*. Mom and Dad must have contacted her to ask for help. These books were a way for their little alliance to communicate without being discovered. Low-tech always trumps high-tech. At least that's what Dad says.

I laughed out loud. "No *wonder* Mrs. H is such a bad teacher."

"Ahem." Dad was standing in the doorway, looking at me grimly.

I jumped up, scattering books everywhere. "I can explain!" I said, rushing toward him.

He held up his hand. "Stop."

"But, Dad!" I protested. "I was just trying to find out what's going on—why you and Mom are always acting so strange. I just wanted to—"

Dad crossed his arms over his chest. "I respect that you're curious, Mike, but rifling through someone else's private things is unacceptable."

"But, Dad! The sabotage—I found your code! I found your messages! Are we really going to try to save Hubble? Are you and Mom going after the *Spirit*?" My heart soared as I realized what this all would mean: No more teasing in school. No more mean looks at my family as we passed by people in town.

"You . . . you did what?" Dad asked.

"How did you find out?" I asked, giddy with the revelations. "How did you find out the *Spirit* wasn't vaporized? Is that why the ship is moving to the Fold right now? Are we going to find the *Spirit*?"

Mom appeared behind Dad in the doorway. "What is he talking about, Albert?"

A faint smile grew on Dad's face. He looked at me like he was seeing me for the first time. "Apparently our son has cracked the poem code."

*"What?"* Mom's mouth lolled open.

I reached down and grabbed some of the ripped-out pages, thrusting them at Mom and Dad. "What does this part mean?" I asked excitedly. "The part about Aurora's hand in sabotage? The virus?"

Mom and Dad just stared at me like I had grown horns or something.

"I mean," I continued rapidly, "this morning Nita kept saying something about Aurora but I couldn't understand her."

Mom shook her head like she was trying to clear water from her ears. "What did you just say?"

Dad blinked a couple of times and then said, "You talked to—"

"Yes!" I said, feeling exasperated, wanting them to start answering my questions. "I talked to Nita. I hacked into her com-bracelet this morning. . . . I saw her. She's fine. But if she's undercover with the EFEs, why wouldn't she have just contacted you guys? Can you please tell me—?"

"Michael Newton Stellar." Mom's voice was dangerously steady and she spoke through gritted teeth. "Why in Heaven's name didn't you tell us at once—"

"She told me not to, Mom. She said . . ." I swallowed and then I spoke as quickly as I could, feeling a cold sweat break out on my palms and under my arms. "She said you and Dad were sabotaging the trip to Mars. She tried to tell me more, but the connection was so bad I couldn't understand her very well. She said things about David Hazelwood and Aurora. And danger. And she finally shouted, 'Mom and Dad are in on the sabotage.' "

Mom put her hand on my shoulder.

"Michael, honey, of course we're in on the sabotage. We're the ringleaders."

27

**At first I** thought I'd missed something.

"Uh, what now?"

"The sabotage," Dad said. He shook his head. "Well, it's a mission redirection, really. Nita's right. We've been planning this for months. She's been helping us."

"I'm so glad you talked to her," Mom said. "We've been trying to contact her ever since we got on the ship but someone's been blocking our transmission."

"But you guys are definitely the good guys, aren't you?"

"Yes, Mike, we're the good guys. Now, what did Nita tell you? I don't understand why she—"

Mr. Shugabert's disembodied voice interrupted and made us all jump. "Attention. You have a visitor. To let him or her enter, just say 'Yes.' "

We all looked at each other and shouted, "NO!" at the same time.

A voice from outside the door stated, "Security override! Move away from the door!"

Suddenly the door exploded open and four men burst into the room. Two of them grabbed Mom and Dad, and Mr. Shugabert reached for my arm. I wriggled away from his grasp and darted around the room, trying to evade capture.

One man stepped into the room and watched the melee grimly. He began to recite something as the two men holding Mom and Dad steered them toward the front door.

"You are under arrest for the planning and partial execution of a devious and illegal plot to thwart the official mission of the Project's *Sojourner* Mars Expedition. . . ."

That was all I heard as I slipped through Mr. Shugabert's hands and ran through the open door. Thinking quickly, I reached into my pocket and pulled out a loose grasshrinker. I hopped onto the tree outside our apartment door and smashed the grasshrinker onto the trunk, careful not to get any of the exposed juice on my hand. In a flash, the tree was half its size and I easily hopped to the lobby floor below. The tree shrunk so fast Mr. Shugabert didn't have time to jump on after me. I had a good head start now.

Running as fast as I could, I glanced over my shoulder and saw his dark figure scrambling down the stairs. I ran blindly, not knowing where to go. I was on a spaceship, for donkey's sake, so the hiding places were limited.

Suddenly Larc came from around a corner and grabbed my arm. She yoinked me back around the corner with her, keeping us out of Sugar Bear's sight.

She dragged me along a corridor until we popped out in the lobby, right next to the secret hallway. "We need to get down there . . . ," she whispered fiercely. I reached into my pocket and pulled out Mr. Shugabert's handheld.

"Remember this?" I asked with a smile. I turned it on and began scrolling through files.

Larc squealed and said, "Well, find the code! Hurry!"

I scrolled and scrolled, but it was too late. We saw Mr. Shugabert and two other guys running full speed toward us.

"We'd better run!" Larc shouted.

"Wait!" I said, staring at the keypad, trying to figure out what to do. "Oh, this'll be mega cool if it works," I said, and I punched the keypad as hard as I could.

Nothing.

I punched it again.

"Come on, Mike!" Larc said, and she whipped past me.

"Larc! Wait!" I shouted, because the keypad had started beeping. I couldn't believe my thug approach had worked!

But it didn't work. The beeping degenerated into a kind of low honking, and smoke wisped out of the keypad.

"You broke it!" screeched Larc.

I rubbed my sore knuckles and worried that maybe Larc was right. Then all of a sudden she roughly pushed me aside.

"Stand back!" Larc shouted.

I saw Sugar Bear approaching rapidly and he looked really, really mad. He was barreling down on us like a train. I couldn't look away—until I saw a glimmer out of the corner of my eye. Turning quickly, I thought I saw Larc holding up her hand as a very thin metal tube shot out of her fingertip into the keypad. Practically a millisecond later the rod shot back into her fingertip. I shook my head. Had I really just seen that? I didn't have time to figure it out. The keypad chimed just as Mr. Shugabert growled and reached out for my arm. I threw the stolen handheld and hit him square on the nose. He snarled and grabbed for me again. I was batting his arms away and pressing Larc against the door leading to the hallway. We were cornered. Then the chime on the keypad stopped beeping and the door opened. Larc and I practically fell into the hallway and we scrambled to shut the door behind us.

28

I kept stumbling as I ran. After a few seconds, the blue glow surrounded us and we ran even harder.

There was shouting behind us and the sounds of running feet. Lots of running feet. We came to what looked like a dead end, and Larc smashed her hand into a small button and we tumbled into a circular room.

I fell back into a padded seat that farted when I sat down. Larc was running around like a crazy woman, banging buttons and flipping switches. The shouting was getting louder by the second and so were the slapping footsteps. But then there was a loud *whoosh* and the door clicked shut. The low hum that had surrounded us since we'd entered the hallway became an insistent whine, increasing in pitch until I winced and had to hold my ears. The sound made me squint my eyes.

Instinctively, I shouted, "Belt!" A harness wrapped around my shoulders and lap.

Then the whole room around us seemed to explode. We were bathed in blue light, and the screeching sound of metal on metal made me clench my jaw. A huge thrust pushed me back into my seat and I thought of the g-forces from the shuttle trip up to the *Sojourner*.

Then, as suddenly as the noise and the light and the g-forces had begun, they were gone. The only sounds were my haggard breathing and a few beeps. My peapod, a forgotten grasshrinker, and the pages from Mrs. H's book were floating in front of me. My ears were itchy from my weightless hair dancing around them. I reached up, snatched everything from the air, and stuffed it all back into my pockets. I swallowed and patted my hair.

"What did you just do?" I frantically asked the back of the chair in front of me. "Your finger! This pod! *What did you do?*"

The chair turned and wild white hair whipped around Larc's pale face. Her blue braces beamed at me.

"I just thought we would hide in here—not *fly away*!" I looked crazily around the pod. Through the porthole next to me, I saw stars streaking by.

Larc giggled and said, "Belt." Her belt slid off and she hovered in front of me. With her hair whipping around and her billowing jumpsuit, she looked like a ghost or a fairy or something.

"An escape pod is for escaping, Mike. It's not called a *hiding pod*."

"But where are we going?" I asked sharply. "Belt!" I floated out of my seat and floundered my way closer to her. "The goons have my parents. We have to go back, we have to—"

"We're not going back," Larc said very matter-of-factly, and she floated over to the console in front of her chair. She pointed to a screen with a blipping dot. "The course is charted, Mike."

"What course?" I asked.

"The course to the Fold, silly."

I sputtered, "The *Fold*? We can't go through the Fold in this! We don't have a thick enough hull! Are you insane?" I had a funny feeling in my cheeks and then realized that it wasn't my cheeks. It was my throat and stomach.

"I'm gonna hurl," I choked out. Larc handed me a bag. I took a few deep breaths and calmed myself without puking. I handed the empty bag back to Larc. "I need some of that stomach-settling vitamin stuff from Dad. . . ."

Larc looked at me and cocked her head. "You don't know anything, do you, Mike?"

I didn't know if she meant about life in general, about almost barfing, or about the ship.

"My dad told me you were in trouble. He sent me to find you and get you off the ship. He said the mission was compromised. This little trip wasn't supposed to happen for another few days, but with your parents captured . . . I would have said something, but I wasn't supposed to tell you about any of—"

"Can you tell me *now, before I have to strangle you*?" I shouted.

"Fine, fine," Larc said, floating away from me. "You don't have to get violent." She took a deep breath. "Remember how we saw all those people on my monitor a few weeks ago?"

"The blinky-dot map?"

"No, dummy, the other thing. The actual people. In actual apartments. Talking."

"Yeah," I said gruffly. "I remember."

"Well, our monitor turned on again this evening and it showed you guys being dragged out of your apartment. Your parents must have pushed an emergency transceiver.

"And when I told Ji—Dad—about Sugar Bear and how it seemed like he was a spy, and how you *accused* him of being one right to his face, well, Dad was going to warn your father. He actually made an emergency appointment so their meeting wouldn't seem suspicious."

I squinched my eyes. "So Sugar Bear must have called up the goons as soon as I opened my big mouth. He must have had our apartment under surveillance the whole time." I shivered.

"Something like that. At least, that's what my dad thought when he saw the arrests."

I thought about everything for a minute. My puzzle was finally almost complete.

"I thought you'd be happy that I helped get you out of trouble." Larc pouted.

I gestured around the pod. "*This* is getting me out of trouble? I'm surprised a hundred of these pods aren't out trying to rein us back in."

Larc snorted dismissively. "Oh, I'm sure the ship's under lockdown by now. The Project thugs are probably rounding people up for questioning. I bet no one even knows we're gone except for Sugar Bear and the other guys we escaped from—and who are they going to want to brag about *that* to?"

I felt a little panicky, but I did my best to stifle it. "So what's our plan? Where are we going?"

Larc grinned. "I already told you, Mike. The course is set."

"What course?"

"We're continuing the mission. We're going to find the *Spirit*."

**That's when I** turned a little green again.

Larc smiled as my face returned to its regular color. "Oh, yeah . . . that 'stomach-settling' vitamin serum your dad kept giving you? That was really a trace amount of radium. Nothing to hurt you; it was just a marker. That way your parents would be able to track your movements and always know where you were. Every member of the sabotage crew was marked."

"*That* was the blinky-dot map we saw in your apartment," I said breathlessly.

She reached over and patted my back. "Yep. So no help with nervous queasiness, I'm afraid. The vitamin stuff never actually had any vitamins in it at all."

"Great," I said. "Next you'll tell me that you're really

an alien sent from another galaxy to help prevent the destruction of your home planet."

Larc looked at me very calmly and then broke into a huge smile. She cocked her head to the side and said, "Weeeeeelllll . . . now that you mention it . . ."

My mouth fell open. I *knew* her white hair was abnormal! I started to say something when she let out a guffaw and slapped me on the back.

"I'm not an *alien!*" She was laughing pretty hard now. "But I had you going, didn't I?"

"Ha-ha," I said, not laughing.

Larc's white hair brushed my face as she roughly pushed past me and stared out the window.

"Hey," I said. "Watch ou—"

But Larc cut me off. Her voice was frantic. "Shut up, stupid. Can't you see? It's the Fold. Already! We're coming up on it too fast." She pushed past me again, this time moving the other way, and she tried furiously pounding controls at the front of the pod.

"Let me help," I said, awkwardly pushing off my seat to float toward her.

"You don't know how to pilot this ship!" she said frantically as she continued to whack at buttons.

"Neither do you!" I retorted. "I've at least had a few years playing ship simulators."

"No, Mike. You don't understand . . . it's on autopilot. Oh, man, it's going to get bumpy in here."

200

I harrumphed angrily and pulled myself down into my seat. "Belt," I muttered. Who was she to get all bossy all of a sudden? *I* was the bossy one. As soon as my belt clicked, though, the pod rolled violently upside down and I was glad to have my seat belt on. Larc banged her head on the controls hard enough to make me wince just from the sound of it.

"Are you okay?" I shouted over the alarms coming from the controls. "Your head," I said, pointing to the gash on her forehead.

She made a face and reached up and felt along the jagged edges of the cut. It wasn't bleeding but it really looked like it should be.

"I'm fine!" she shouted back. "Hold on!"

The pod righted itself and started to dive backward. It was gaining speed so quickly that we could hear the metal of the hull groaning and creaking.

"The Fold is sucking us in, isn't it?" I shouted over the noise.

"It's a strong one, all right. The plasma-propulsion cells still need to finish powering up!"

Larc didn't seem panicked, but she was very brisk with her words. She still wasn't buckled in and was fruitlessly pushing and flipping and twisting controls right and left with her feet sticking straight out behind her.

"If I could just . . . ," she said, grasping a thin

joystick-like thing that was sticking up from the floor in front of the controls. She fought with the stick, grunting and pulling.

"Let me help you," I hollered over the twisting metallic noise that was growing louder and louder. I unbuckled my seat belt and propelled myself to her side. We both heaved and pulled. Larc gave one last grunt and I gave a sharp kick and the stick jammed into the floor of the pod, sinking out of view. The pod immediately slowed down and stopped spinning. We could see the outer edges of the Fold approaching, but at a much slower, much safer pace.

Wiping her hair from her forehead, Larc said, "There. Manual override."

I stared at her, dumbfounded. "You must play simulators, too."

She shrugged. "It's kind of intuitive."

Larc finally pulled herself down into her seat and said, "Belt." She didn't look tired, but she did look anxious.

"How are you feeling?" she asked. "You're not still below the weather, are you?"

I smiled sheepishly. "*Under* the weather? No. I think I'm okay now."

"Good," she said. "Because it's about to get pretty crazy in here."

"What do you mean?"

"We have a— Hey, look!"

The ship was entering the Fold now and streaks of color flew by. One particular streak was light blue and moving almost parallel to our pod.

"It's the heat signature of the *Spirit*," I said in awe. "At least, I think it is. I've read that when ships fly through Folds, they leave a wake of—"

"You're right," Larc said. "It's pretty faint after two years, but it's there. We're definitely on the right track."

I barely heard her. I had never seen anything like it. The colors were so vibrant, almost three-dimensional. It was like being inside the brightest rainbow I'd ever seen. I found myself thinking of Mom and how much she would love to see this. I wondered what was happening to her and Dad.

"They'll be fine," Larc said, floating up behind me and looking out the window with me. "As long as we get back in time, everything will be fine."

"Get back? I thought you said we weren't going back."

"Well, *eventually* we're going back, Mike. But we need David Hazelwood and Hubble and the rest of the *Spirit* crew first."

"I don't think they're going to fit in this pod," I said, trying a joke to lighten my mood.

"Probably not," Larc replied with a grin. "But I bet we can work something out."

The colors were flying by and it suddenly started to sink in that we were really on our way to the *Spirit* . . . or what was left of it.

"You're going to really want to hold on to the seat of your pants, Mike," Larc said, interrupting my thoughts.

I watched her curiously as she flexed the fingers of her right hand and then held her palm out like she was going to grab my face. I could see the ugly bluish star-shaped scar. The vein in the middle of it was throbbing.

She smiled and said, "Buckled in tight?"

I chewed my lip and answered, "Yeah, but what are you doing?" And she came at me with her palm sticking straight out in front of her.

"Not that crazy finger thing again!" I said, and dodged my head out of her way, but she wasn't really coming at me. She floated past me to a small indentation on the wall. I had guessed it was just another control or light switch or something, but now, as I looked at it, I saw that it had the same shape as the scar on her hand.

"Hold on to your britches, Mike," she said. "This is going to be wild." And she pressed her palm onto the indentation.

Nothing happened. She took her hand away from the wall, shook it fiercely, and then matched her scar back up with the groove. Still nothing. She squinched up her face in frustration and then her eyes widened.

"It's shorted out," she said almost imperceptibly. "From you!" She jabbed the air at me.

"What's shorted out?" I asked, confused. "I didn't touch anything!"

"My hand!" she shouted. "Your sweat from holding it! The Wormer is toast!"

"Mother of donkeys, Larc, what are you *talking about*?"

Then it was almost as if I could actually hear a *ding!* announcing that she had an idea.

"Come here," she commanded.

I looked at her out of the corner of my eye. "What are you doing?"

"Just *come here* or we're going to *miss it*!" she shouted.

I floated over to her and she grabbed my shoulder. Hard. "Turn your head to the side," she ordered. Then, when I was too slow, she grabbed my head with her free hand and twisted it so that my ear was facing her instead of my face. "Don't move."

"What are you . . . ? *Ow!*" I felt a white-hot shot of pain in my ear, and then a millisecond later it was gone.

"Thanks," Larc said. "Now hold on for your life."

**30**

**Before I even** had a chance to try to figure out why the scar on Larc's hand matched the indentation on the wall of the pod, or what she had done to my ear, or why she had been yelling at me, we were engulfed in light. I scrambled to my seat and yelled, "Belt!" I pulled it extra tight.

The pod flew upward like we were in a plasma-charged elevator. Then it went down. Then to the left and to the right and to the left again. The only thing I could see was a brightness that swallowed everything. Yet something about the brightness curved in, like we were shooting through an insane waterslide.

I could hear Larc shouting, "Hold on! Just a few more minutes!"

Those few minutes felt like dog years, but eventually

the brightness dimmed and the pod stopped lurching. Larc's arm fell from the wall and she gave me a tired smile.

"Wormhole," she said. "What a ride."

I stammered, "That was a . . . We just went through a . . ."

"A wormhole, Mike," she said, floating past me, her arm flopping limply at her side. "A shortcut through space . . . just like a worm taking a shortcut from one side of an apple to another. It's *way* faster than going all the way around the apple. Though maybe a little bumpier." She smiled and then pointed at me. "You almost ruined it, you know. But then, thankfully . . . well, you didn't."

I didn't know what to say, except "Your hand is smoking."

Sure enough, little wisps of smoke were rising from her palm. Larc didn't say anything; she just rubbed her hand on her jumpsuit and the smoking stopped.

Looking out the window, I noticed we weren't in the Fold anymore. In fact, there was no Fold to be seen anywhere. There were millions of stars and, in the distance, a small red planet.

Larc said, "Aries. Once we get a little closer, we should see the *Spirit* in a high orbit."

"But I thought the *Spirit* was going to Mars," I said, confused.

"They were, Mike, but Aurora hijacked their course and sent them out here to no-man's-land, where she thought they'd never be discovered."

I didn't say anything. I didn't think I could.

Larc pulled herself down into her chair and smiled. She was being suspiciously quiet. I floated up behind her and watched out the front window. Slowly, the planet Aries began to grow larger and larger as we moved closer to it. It looked similar to Mars, but there were patches of green—and black—among the different colors of red.

As our pod gracefully propelled toward the planet, I saw a silver shimmer. As its orbit brought it closer to us, we could just barely make out the *Spirit*. It had an eerie resemblance to the *Sojourner*.

"That's it," I whispered. "The *Spirit*. Man, it looks beat up." There were pockmarks all along the side, and there were areas that had been blackened by something.

"Shouldn't we hail them?" I asked, reaching for the buttons on the control panel.

"I'm already on it," Larc said with a sparkle in her eye.

After a few seconds there was a loud buzz from the controls.

"That should be them," Larc said, pressing a green button. "*Spirit*, this is the *Liberator*. Do you copy?"

A crackly voice filled the cabin. "Over, *Liberator*.

We hear you loud and clear." Larc beamed at me, and I pulled myself down into my chair, stunned. Over and over in my head, I kept hearing "This is really happening. . . . This is really happening."

"We're coming in at delta speed, *Spirit*, right up on your portside flap."

"Perfect," the crackly voice said. "We'll dust off the extractor and bring you in."

Then I had a thought: the *Spirit* didn't seem overly surprised to hear from us, and I would think they'd be freaking out to hear the voices of another ship after two years. It was as if they'd known we were coming.

"If you haven't figured it out by now," Larc said, turning around in her chair and facing me, "the *Spirit* already knew we were coming."

I gave a weak smile.

"Our parents have been communicating with the *Spirit* for months now, planning this rescue."

I blinked a few times and looked at Larc. "They must have been communicating in secret, though. 'Cause nothing in my dad's books—the codes—there was nothing about public communication."

"Well, people know they've been *trying* to communicate with the *Spirit*, but no one knows the *Spirit* has actually been answering."

"How could they not know? Wouldn't they hear or read the transmissions?"

"Oh, Mike, our parents are smarter than that! The *Spirit* has been sending encoded messages to the sabotage team. The code sounds and looks like—"

I snapped my fingers. "Static! It has to be static, right? Low-tech trumps high-tech."

"Spot on, Sherlock," Larc said, making an A-OK sign with her hand.

That totally explained why all our electrical appliances at home had seemed like they were on the fritz. I knew there was something crazy about the viserator shooting whorls of static for so long!

The pod lurched forward and we were bathed in a faint golden light while the grappling ray moved us steadily toward the *Spirit*. I was excited but 100 percent freaked out at the same time. The moment I'd wished for for two years was actually happening and I was sick with apprehension.

The pod bumped into the massive hull of the *Spirit* and an opening appeared. We clattered through a narrow tube and came to rest in a small circular alcove. The golden light disappeared and was replaced by the blue glow of our ship. A rushing sound filtered through the pod and I felt a sickly sensation in my stomach. My butt sunk into my seat and my hair fell around my ears. I felt the stuff in my pocket settle against my leg. We were back in AutoGrav territory again.

The ship automatically powered down with a kind

of roar-sigh that sounded tired. A door at the far end of the alcove slid open and a man walked toward our pod. He had outstretched arms and a broad smile.

"There he is," Larc said, whipping her hair back into a ponytail and smoothing her jumpsuit. "It's Captain Herschel Winkley."

I watched as she threw herself into the man's arms and hugged him as if he was her long-lost grandfather.

Hesitantly, I climbed out of the pod and walked toward the two of them. They were already immersed in deep conversation and barely noticed when I got there.

After a few seconds Larc said, "Captain Wink, this is my friend Mike Stellar. You know his parents and he knows Hubble. Mike, this is Captain Wink—commander of the *Spirit*."

"Ah, yes," the man said, and I could see now that he was very old. "Michael Stellar. I've heard a lot about you."

"You have?" I asked, not knowing how to respond. "I—I've never heard anything about you. Well, except for all the stuff in the news when the *Spirit* disappeared."

"Mi-ike!" Larc said, laughing.

The old man laughed and patted my shoulder. "Come along now." He swept me and Larc along with his outstretched arms. "We have a lot to accomplish and not a lot of time to accomplish it in."

Before we took another step, though, the door to the

alcove opened again and a man stood there wearing possibly the biggest smile I'd ever seen. Even though he was skinny and wore a beard, I recognized Hubble immediately.

He swept me up in a whirling hug. Then he plopped me down and grabbed my arms. Roughly, he pulled me to him and kissed my forehead with a loud smack.

"Holy mother of donkeys, kid, you're huge! Immense! I mean"—he was turning me around now and laughing—"you look like a gen-u-ine grown-up teenaged kid." He ruffled my hair, then took a step back and looked at me some more.

I was beaming. I didn't know what to say. I couldn't believe it was really him. Hubble. Right in front of me. Talking to me. Alive. Breathing. Hairy.

"Say something, kiddo. Talk to me. How's Yeager? Is he as big as you?"

"Stinky's fine," I said. "He's great—or he will be when he finds out you're okay. He's bigger than me now, can you believe it?"

"How's your sister?" Hubble asked, his face clouding over.

"She's fine, Hubble. She's never given up looking for you, even when everyone said it was no use."

Hubble grabbed me up in another hug. As I hugged him back, I could feel his ribs through his jumpsuit and that kind of brought me back to reality.

"We need to get you home, man," I said, gesturing at him. "You look like you need a good dinner."

"I do, little dude. I surely do." He dropped his arm over my shoulder.

"Come on, you two," Larc said, stepping around us and through the doorway. "We have stuff to do."

**As we walked** quickly through some dark hallways and wound our way up through the belly of the ship, I finally remembered to introduce Larc and Hubble. Hubble gave Larc a hug almost as big as the one he gave me, saying, "I've heard a lot about you." Larc just grinned and said, "Likewise."

"How have you heard a lot about . . . ?" I looked at Hubble quizzically.

"We don't have time to chat," Larc interrupted. "Come on, hurry up!"

"She's right," said Captain Wink. "We'd better shake a leg, you two."

At the same time, Hubble and I both stopped and shook our right legs furiously. His mother had always said "shake a leg," so that was what Stinky and Hubble and I did whenever she said it to us. Really, Hubble acted a lot like a kid in his teens. I always wondered how he'd gotten his job at the Project, even if he *was* a rocket science genius. He's smart, but not a very serious guy.

"Not helping," Larc said over her shoulder. "Let's *go*!"

Hubble took off down the hallway like his pants were on fire. Larc kept pace with him, while Captain Wink and I had to practically jog to keep up.

We arrived at a small, boring-looking door at the end of a hallway. Out of breath, I asked, "Where are we?"

It was a simple question, yet it was met with looks of consternation from everyone. Larc chewed her lip and looked at the ground. Hubble opened his mouth to say something, but no words came out.

I looked at everyone. "What's going on?"

"We're going to try to get home, Mike," Hubble said slowly. "But there's something you need to know about Larc—"

Suddenly the door opened and a small old man stood there. His expression was grim but it brightened as soon as he saw Larc.

He took her hand. "You don't know what it means to us to have you on the ship," he said in a raspy voice.

"It's Jim and Albert and Marie you need to thank," Larc said, walking into the room. "Not me."

I leaned forward, dumbly thinking that by moving

closer to the scene, I would understand what was going on.

"You realize the time frame we're on?" the old man asked as the others filed into the room behind Larc. I followed, mystified.

"*Yes*," Hubble said. He was scratching his head in the way that he does when he's really impatient. I'd seen that move a lot when he was irritated at me and Stinky.

"Well, what's the plan, then, Hubble?" the old man asked, equally impatient.

"The plan is the same as it's always been," Hubble said.

"But what about . . . ?" The old man nodded ever so slightly in my direction.

"Without Mike I would have never made it here," Larc said quickly. "He's part of the mission now, David."

"Fine, then," David said, waving his hand dismissively. "I trust you. Can we please get started now? One more second in orbit of this dreadful planet is one second too long."

Everyone except me looked expectantly at Larc. I was staring at David. I couldn't believe I was in the same room as the famed David Hazelwood. And that he was so *small*. And *old*.

Larc cleared her throat and said, "Well, we have a bit of a problem."

"What is it?" Hubble asked, trying to sound calm.

"I needed help to power through the wormhole. Mike's help, actually."

"Mike?" Hubble asked. "But how? I don't under—"

"That's not the point, Hubble," Larc said, interrupting him. "The point is that my power cells have degenerated. There was a short when some liquid seeped into the Wormer." She held up her scar and poked at it. "I don't think I have enough power to get the *Spirit* back to Earth."

There was dead silence in the room. Finally Hubble said quietly, "How did Mike help with the wormhole?"

"It was his RRE, from a tracking serum administered by Albert and Marie."

"Wait, wait, wait," I said, holding up my hands. "RRE?" I knew what RRE was. We had studied that last semester. "That's residual radioactive energy, right?"

Larc looked at me expectantly.

"I've been drinking that serum a bunch of times a day since we first got on the shuttle. If you need RRE to help with whatever it is you're talking about, then I'm sure I have plenty to spare."

Larc nodded. "It can't hurt to try, can it?"

"Well, if it has anything to do with that finger

thing," I said, involuntarily reaching for my ear, "it probably *is* going to hurt me."

No one said anything for a minute. Then Captain Wink said, "If we're going to give this a shot, we need to get this show on the road—*now*."

**Hubble came over** and stood beside me. I gave him a what-in-the-name-of-donkeys-are-you-doing? look, but I didn't have a chance to say anything, because Larc was talking again.

"First," she said, "sit down, Mike."

I sat. Captain Wink and David stood on either side of me like guards.

"Next," Larc continued, "take this. Jim might want it back. He didn't specify." And she took off her hair.

That's right.

Hair.

Gone.

She handed the mass of white to Hubble, who plopped it onto the table in front of me. I involuntarily flinched and stared at Larc, mouth agape.

"You should probably take this, too," she said, unzipping her jumpsuit.

"Whoa!" I jumped up from the table, turning my back to her and shielding my eyes in one swift movement.

Hubble chuckled and sat me back down. "Nothing to worry about, Mike," he said. I slowly opened my eyes and saw not the naked Larc I was expecting, but a glowing control panel of sorts that seemed to have arms and legs and Larc's bald head sticking out from it. The hands reached up and peeled off Larc's face. They handed it to Hubble, who took the face and plopped it onto the table next to the hair. I swallowed and looked around the room. No one else seemed shocked. Then the now faceless control panel spoke.

It said, "I'm sorry you had to find out this way, Mike. I kept meaning to tell you, but, well, it just never came up in conversation."

"Oh, don't look so shocked, boy," Captain Wink said with a sympathetic smile. "Didn't you ever think Larc was a little too perfect? Knew too much about too many things?"

"Uh," I said. "Well. I never really thought she was perfect."

The Larc/control panel monstrosity hee-hawed in Larc's familiar way. "Thanks a lot, buddy," the control panel said in Larc's voice.

Trying desperately to set aside my absolute shock, I croaked, "So is-is that a petabyte processor or are you just happy to see me?"

The control panel laughed again.

Hubble walked proudly over to the mangle of blinking lights and black wires. "What we have here, Mike, is a very state-of-the-art Liberation and Rescue Cyborg. Or L.A.R.C., as you know it."

The control panel harrumphed.

"Sorry. *Her.* As you know *her,*" Hubble said with a smile. "Larc is a very sophisticated piece of machinery, Mike. She's equipped with the most advanced artificial intelligence, as well as miniaturized plasma-propulsion cells. She's a walking, talking spaceship engine, with a lot of extras.

"It's ingenious, really," Hubble continued as he pushed buttons where Larc's stomach used to be. "Her father, and your parents, knew they needed a way to get our ship moving again if a rescue was going to happen. That's when they thought of smuggling plasma-propulsion cells onto the *Sojourner*."

"So Larc's dad—Jim—figured out how to stuff the cells in a robot," I said quietly as it began to make sense to me.

"A perfect Trojan horse!" David said gleefully. "The whole plan worked perfectly until . . ."

"My sweaty hand shorted out her—what was it?

Wormer?" I asked. "Now her plasma propulsion isn't strong enough to power the wormhole," I finished.

"She's going to be destroyed," David said quietly. "She'll just barely be able to power the *Spirit* out of here."

Hubble stopped pushing buttons and said, "I'm sorry, man. That wasn't part of the original plan. We've lucked out with your RRE. But even with that she's going to have to use every ounce of energy in her cells to power the *Spirit*. And we won't even make it home. We'll have to stop at the *Sojourner* and bunk in with you guys."

I had a sinking feeling. "I don't know if that's—"

Captain Wink cut me off. "I trust you and Larc have said your good-byes, because the time is upon us." He glanced at the clock on the wall. "Our window is here." He walked over to Hubble and helped him with the last bit of button pushing.

Now that I knew Larc was a robot, a lot of things started making sense. No wonder she knew so much about the ship and the escape pod. And the glowing blue braces and blue veins under her skin must have been the plasma energy charging. Being a robot was a pretty good excuse for never eating or drinking anything. And it also explained why she couldn't scan her eyeball to open her apartment door, and why her forehead hadn't bled when she'd whacked it in the escape pod.

I shook my head in disbelief at my utter, well, *belief* of the situation. Of all the weird things to happen in the past few weeks, this one made the most sense. And David was right. Creating a robot to hide the fuel cells was ingenious. It made me think of my parents in a whole new light.

I walked up to Captain Wink and Hubble . . . and Larc, who was being trussed into some kind of closet at the back of the room. Captain Wink plugged Larc into several outlets in the wall. Her fingers snapped in here, a foot over there. . . . It was a very complicated process. By the time he finished, Larc didn't even have a human form anymore. I could just barely make out where her face had been. It was the cool glow of the still-present braces that tipped me off.

"So you need my ear, don't you?" I asked, feeling a surprising sense of pride.

"It's really very simple," Hubble said. He took one of Larc's free fingers and tapped the tip. Her fingertip opened like a hinged lid, and a thin metal rod slid out about twelve inches. "This rod will channel your RRE into Larc. Hopefully it will jump-start her plasma propulsion, just like it did for the wormhole. It'll only hurt for a second."

I closed my eyes and said, "Go for it."

"Here goes nothing," Hubble said, and I felt the quick searing pain. I rolled my eyes to the side to see what Hubble was doing. But the rod was already sliding out of my ear.

"All done," he said, replacing Larc's fingertip and snapping the finger into a small hole in the wall. "Anything you want to say to her before she powers up?"

I just stood there for a moment, staring at the mass of wires and blinking lights. It still wasn't really registering that this was Larc. My friend. Even though I'd seen what had happened to her, I still couldn't believe she had dissolved into piles of wires and chips. I felt awkward trying to talk to a mass of circuitry. It was weird.

"Sorry I acted like an idiot most of the time," I said to the braces. "You were a good friend. Weird and everything, but now I guess I know why. And you helped me out a lot, which I appreciate. And . . . well, good-bye, I guess. Have fun doing whatever it is you're about to do." I reached out my hand to touch the braces, but Captain Wink held me back.

"Ooh, I'd think twice about that, Mike," came Larc's voice, sounding buzzy and hoarse. "I promise you don't want the magnetic energy I'm creating right now to give you a zap."

"No," I said, withdrawing my hand. "No. I guess not."

"Well, then, it's time we got this boat a-rockin'," Hubble said, slapping me on the back. "I'm gonna flick this switch here and we'll be on our way. Larc is gonna get us back to the *Sojourner* just fine."

"About that . . . ," I said hesitantly, giving the blue braces one last look. "The *Sojourner* may have already turned around by now. My parents, Larc's dad . . . creator . . . whatever—they may all be in jail. Or worse."

"How's that?" Hubble asked distractedly, jamming his hand onto a big red button. The contorted mass that used to be Larc's body lurched and then started glowing a bright blue.

"I thought they were expecting us," David said. The room began to hum loudly. I instinctively sat down and said, "Belt," but the *Spirit* was too old to have voice-activated seat belts. The humming grew louder and louder and finally I grabbed the strap and pulled it tightly over my lap.

"Well, they are expecting us," I said, raising my voice over the growing hum, "but it's probably a different 'they' than you think."

33

**Even the crazy** ups and downs and brain-rattling curves didn't stop me from arguing with Hubble all the way through the Fold. And he STILL wouldn't listen to me. He took me aside and put his hand on my arm. Quietly, he said, "Mike, I understand that you're a little freaked out right now."

"I've been through the Fold *twice,* Hubble!" I shouted, my stomach still churning from the second time. "*Twice in one day!* Plus wormholes! Of *course* I'm freaked out!" I wanted to grab him by the throat and throttle him. "But just because I'm freaked out doesn't mean I don't know what I'm talking about!"

"I understand you are concerned, Mike, but you need to just let us carry out our plan, okay?" Hubble continued calmly. "We'll make sure your parents are safe. Once they're safe, we'll worry about everything else. All right?"

I could feel my eyebrows go as pointy as they'd ever been. I'd just spent what felt like hours explaining to Hubble and Captain Wink and David what was happening on the *Sojourner*. Even as we felt the *Spirit* attain air lock with the *Sojourner*, I repeated, in detail, how evil Mr. Shugabert was and how he would stop at nothing to prevent my parents from saving the people on the *Spirit*. And now Hubble was telling me to stay out of it. To let the big boys do the fighting.

"Don't talk to me like I'm a baby, Hubble," I growled. "I want to help. I need to help. I'm the only one who's seen what these goons can do—"

"Mike," Hubble said, turning from the computer terminal where he'd been accessing the security cameras on the *Sojourner*. "Listen. After everything I've been through—after everything *you've* been through—I just can't let you get hurt. I will not be responsible for putting you in any more danger. Plus, I need you to stay here. Help us from the flight deck. I've asked Meridiani here to assist you."

A rumble of throat clearing came from the doorway. I turned and saw a gigantic man with a bald head shining, even under the low, sick light of the *Spirit*. His flight suit was tattered, but it still clung to the muscles on his arms.

"*That* guy?" I frowned. "He's supposed to *assist* me?"

Meridiani crossed the room and put a heavy hand on my shoulder.

"Don't cause trouble, Mike," Hubble said shortly. "Just stay here on the ship. Once things are settled, we'll come for you. Besides, if something was really wrong, we'd know about it. We've had weekly updates from Albert and Marie and Jim and Venus for almost a full year now. If something was sketchy, they would have let us know during our last contact."

"When was your last contact?" I spat.

Hubble sighed. "A couple of days ago, Mike. Don't worry about it." He ran his hand through his beard. "We're taking precautions, okay? We're armed. We're ready for anything they might throw at us. Plus, we've already contacted the ship. See? They're sending some guys to meet us at the air lock." He motioned to the terminal screen. It showed an image of four black-suited men marching down the *Sojourner* air lock hallway.

"But, Hubble, those are *bad dudes*. And there are a billion times more than four of those guys on the ship."

"You still have a tendency to exaggerate, don't you, kiddo?" Hubble laughed. "We may be a little scraggly, but the *Spirit* crew is still more than seventy-five strong. We outnumber those guys."

"This is all such a load of—" I said, disgusted. "They all have *weapons*, Hubble! They—"

"Don't worry, I'm not going to let you down." Hubble typed a few commands and some more security camera images appeared. He frowned when he saw several huge men walking down a hallway. He turned and looked at me. "Don't *you* let us down, either. Stay here, big guy. We need you to monitor the air lock connection with Meridiani."

Hubble tapped the terminal screen with his finger, turning it off. He stood up, hugged me, and walked after David and Captain Wink, who had already left the room and started down the hall toward the air lock. I could hear the crowds of *Spirit* crew members waiting to join them as they boarded the *Sojourner*.

" 'Big guy'?" I shouted after him. " *'Big guy'?!*" Meridiani grabbed my shoulder to steer me out of the room. Hubble, David, and Captain Wink were already out of sight but I tore loose from Meridiani's grip and ran, trying to catch up to them. As soon as I made it to the air lock, the door slid shut. It had no keypad. Just like the rest of the *Spirit*'s doors, it required an actual key. No chance to hack into it. Low-tech always trumps high-tech.

Breathing heavily, I slumped against the closed air lock. This Meridiani guy wasn't going to assist me with anything. He was just a babysitter . . . maybe even a bodyguard or something.

I sunk my head onto my knees. What was I going to

do? Just sit there and wait for them all to be creamed? Even with what was left of the *Spirit* crew, they were easily outnumbered two to one. And with the strength of the Project goons compared to the raggedy-ass weaklings these slop-eating *Spirit* crew members had become . . . it wasn't even going to be close.

I looked up. Meridiani had found me. His hands were placed tightly at his hips.

"Get up and come with me," he said sternly.

We walked to the flight deck and Meridiani pulled out a chair for me. "Watch that screen," he said stiffly. "If this level goes into the red part, you holler. Got it?"

I just glared at him. He was having way more fun bossing me around than he should have.

It had been about a half hour since Hubble and everyone had left. I was still staring at the stupid air lock monitor, doing absolutely nothing to help. Meridiani was on the other side of the room, cleaning out his ears with a key. I felt a creeping panic and I gripped the slats of my seat, willing myself to stay calm and think.

I decided to find a computer terminal to see if I could still see the *Sojourner*'s security cameras.

"Meridiani! Come quick!" I shouted. "Something's wrong!"

He dropped his keys and came running. Before I could think about it twice, I reached into my pocket and pulled out the extra grasshrinker I'd discovered earlier. I covered my hand with my sleeve and slapped the grasshrinker on the back of Meridiani's neck as he bent down to look at the monitor.

"Sorry, sorry, sorry," I said. "Just don't move and you'll be back to normal in a few minutes. I think." He just stood there, mouth agape. Then, in a blink, he was two feet shorter. Then another two feet, and another. He stood barely eight inches off the ground now. I picked him up and put him next to the air lock monitor. "I really am sorry," I said as I moved to the other side of the room and used his dropped keys to turn on a mainframe terminal.

## 34

After a few minutes of aimlessly searching the terminal, I still couldn't find any feeds to the security cameras. I didn't know what to do. I wanted Larc to help me. And even though I knew she was toasted, I went to find her.

I busted into the room where Hubble and Captain Wink had plugged Larc into the wall. The blast of heat nearly knocked me down. I saw Larc's tangled mass of wires plugged into the wall. What a mess.

The wires were fused together, smoking. Some of the buttons were melted and dripping onto the floor. The braces had no more blue glow. Larc was just a hulking piece of burning fuses.

"Oh, Larc," I whispered. "Look at you."

For the first time in a while, I felt the whisper of

defeat in my ear. The tears rolled down my cheeks on their own. I was useless to stop them. And I didn't feel like a baby or a coward. I felt ashamed. I was here to save my parents . . . the *Spirit*. And I couldn't. I couldn't move. I felt empty without Larc. Useless.

"Why so blue?" came a strangled mechanical voice. I quickly wiped the tears from my face.

"Get it?" it said.

I looked around me. I hadn't noticed before, but the room was still very faintly glowing blue.

"Larc?" I asked in a constricted voice.

"It's grim, Mike. Grim. My processor is fried. All of me is fried." Her voice was rising and lowering in pitch at random intervals.

"Mother of donkeys, Larc." My voice cracked.

"I'm spent, Mike. I can talk to you until my processor goes, but that'll be any minute."

"But I need your help. Everyone's gone. They've been on the *Sojourner* for hours. I don't know what to do next."

"Talk it out, Mike. You're smart. You'll think of something."

I rubbed my face with my hands and I remembered why I'd come into the room. "The security cameras . . . let me see if I can still access them. Maybe that will give us an idea. . . ."

I flipped on the terminal. I traced the programs

233

accessed by the last user and after a few agonizing seconds the screen buzzed to life. I saw a list of *Sojourner* security cameras scrolling down the screen. I randomly clicked on a camera but it didn't show anything. I clicked on another and . . . my worst fears were confirmed. There was fighting in the hallways. Fighting in the lobby. Fighting on the flight deck. And the *Spirit* crew was outnumbered horribly. My fingers shaking, I clicked the link to the brig camera. It showed the brig quickly filling to capacity. It looked like everyone from the *Spirit* had been captured, was in the process of getting captured—or worse.

There was no one left to keep fighting.

No one but me.

"They're in the brig," I choked out. "Well, the ones who aren't already there will be soon. Everyone. From *both* ships."

"Where is the brig?" Larc asked matter-of-factly.

"In the bottom of the ship, I guess. I haven't been down there."

"Can you see if all the Project goons are there, too?"

I clicked on a bunch of different cameras placed throughout the *Sojourner*. "Some are still fighting but most of the goons are down with the prisoners. Hang on. . . ."

I saw a clot of thugs leaving the brig.

"It looks like they might be splitting up."

"Can you hear anything they're saying?"

I tried a couple of commands. "No. The feed Hubble tapped into isn't equipped with sound."

"Can you see where they're all going?" Larc's voice was fading in and out now.

"Looks like they're headed up some stairs. What do you think? Maybe toward the air lock?"

"I can't see, Mike," Larc's scary new voice honked. "My optic processor is in a puddle somewhere."

"Well, uh," I replied, not knowing what to say, "if they're headed toward the air lock, I imagine they're coming to find anyone who's left over here and bring them onto the *Sojourner*. Namely, me."

"Can you tell how the brig is set up? Are there individual cells or what?" Larc's voice was now a mechanical drone.

"It looks like light bars to me. The kind that zap you if you touch them."

"Electric—" Larc's voice buzzed, and then was silent.

"Larc?" I shouted, jumping up. "Larc!"

The blue glow in the room was gone.

Larc was gone.

I could still hear her voice in my head, though. "Talk it out, Mike. Talk it out."

So I did.

There was a fast-approaching cell of goons heading

for the air lock. The rest of them were in the brig with the prisoners. I stared at the terminal screen. After the split-up, the goons in the brig were way outnumbered by prisoners. If I could figure out a way to help the adults get past the light bars, then they'd have a good fighting chance.

But how could they get through the light bars? I ran my hand over the terminal and it shocked me.

"Stupid compu—" I grumped, and then it hit me. It was so obvious!

If the power failed, the light bars would fail. And the brig probably had its own power source. I felt my pulse quicken. The brig's power would have to fail. But how?

Some movement on the screen in front of me caught my attention. The thugs were heading closer and closer to the air lock. They'd be on the *Spirit* in minutes.

35

I needed to figure out how to turn the power off in the brig. That was the only way to disable those light bars. I paced in front of Larc's burnt-out remnants and talked to myself. I must have looked like a raving lunatic.

How could I cut the brig's power source? I sat at the computer terminal to see if I could call up anything that would help—maybe a map, anything. The only even possibly helpful file I found was a copy of the *Spirit*'s blueprints.

My only hope was that the *Spirit* and the *Sojourner* had similar layouts. They were designed by the same woman (Mom and Dad had had her over for dinner once. She was very old and kind of cranky), so it was a good bet. I looked over the blueprints and found the *Spirit*'s brig. Off to one side was its electrical box.

"Huzzah," I said to myself. As long as the *Sojourner* brig's electrical box was in the same place, I was in luck. But how could I get to it? I stared at the melted tangle of Larc and had a crazy idea. I tried to ignore it, but the more I tried to make it go away, the stronger it got.

There was no way I'd get around the goons in the brig to get to the electrical box. But if I could get to the box from the *outside* . . . I could burn through the first layer of the hull and destroy some of the wires. If I did it right, I wouldn't bust through the habitat layer of the hull and kill everyone. If I did it right, I could kill the brig's power instead, and help my parents and Hubble and everyone escape.

If.

If.

If.

I ran to the flight deck at warp speed. I knew that the Project goons would board the ship any second now.

Meridiani was sitting by the air lock monitor. He was a bit bigger than I had left him. The grasshrinker was wearing off. I was relieved and dismayed at the same time. As soon as he saw me, he started shouting words I'd only heard by accidentally flipping to the grown-up channels on the viserator. His little head was beet red. It looked like it might pop off at any second.

"Sorry, sorry, sorry!" I yelled to him as I crossed the room. "I didn't have a choice." He shook his tiny fists at me and squeaked some more obscenities.

I stood next to the spacewalk capsule and took a breath. The capsule looked exactly the same as the one the *Sojourner*'s captain had used when we'd accidentally busted each other breaking the rules. I opened the door, and with a loud *whoosh*, I was inside.

I stood in the capsule, breathing hard. I took one of the suits from its hook and pulled it on. I briefly thought of the report I'd written on the early days of spaceflight and I was so glad that our space suits weren't those bulky monstrosities the first astronauts used.

The slim suit I wore over my flight suit was too big, but it wasn't bad. I flipped on the oxygen tank and the jet pack. Fortunately, they both had easy-to-read diagrams. The oxygen tank had a monitor on the sleeve of the suit, and the jet pack was controlled with simple voice instructions. I struggled to get the helmet properly aligned with all the grooves on the neck of the suit, but I heard a nice click and the helmet said, "Flight ready." I lumbered over to a small cabinet and yanked it open. Inside, there were a plasma torch, some completely unrecognizable tools, an extra jet pack, and a first-aid kit. I grabbed the plasma torch.

"This shouldn't be too hard," I said, trying to convince myself I wasn't on a suicide mission. "Just like playing Astro Wars on the vis." All the spit in my mouth dried up and I briefly thought about forgetting the whole thing. Instead, I ran over the plan one last time, said a quick prayer, and reached for the hatch. I pushed the big button, and yellow warning lights began flashing in the capsule. A mechanical woman's voice counted down from ten to one. I tried to take deep breaths to calm myself, but I was pretty much gulping air. I looked at my oxygen meter—enough to last me twenty minutes. "That should be plenty of time," I told myself. Man, I hoped so.

The voice reached one and the hatch slowly opened. As soon as it began to open, the AutoGrav in the capsule shut off and I started floating. At first I instinctively fought it and I grabbed for the smooth plastic sides of the capsule. As I floated toward the opened hatch, I really felt like I might freak out. What was I doing, going out into space? *Outer space?* The closest thing to a space walk I'd ever experienced was floating around the escape pod with Larc.

Larc.

I missed her. I took a breath and willed myself to stop panicking. I floated effortlessly out of the ship.

I looked around and all I could see was the kind of blackness that seems sticky—like it's clinging to your arms and legs and won't let go.

I could feel my heart rate increase and my breathing turn into huffs and puffs. I was panicking. My head whirled around and I finally noticed that while I was freaking out, I'd floated away from the ships.

"Mo. Ther. Of. Don. *Keys*," I exhaled as I tried to calm myself.

"Everything's okay, Mike," I told myself. "Just simple voice instructions. That's all you need to activate the jet pack." So that was what I did.

"Forward!

"Left!

"Forward!

"Hover!"

It wasn't long before I rubbed my hand along the side of the *Spirit* and breathed a sigh of relief.

By this time my head was pounding with the worst headache I'd had in my entire life. I looked at my oxygen monitor and it showed I had less than five minutes of air to breathe.

"What the . . . !" I cried. "There must be a malfunction with the suit!" I tapped the oxygen monitor stupidly. That, of course, didn't help.

I fought yet another wave of panic and told my jet pack to move forward. I glided away from the *Spirit*, toward the *Sojourner*. It felt like swimming out into the deep end of a pool, only instead of worrying about a drain sucking me under, I worried about black holes and red dwarfs and—

My head still reeled. And my breath was coming in harsh bursts. There was only two and a half minutes before my air would be gone. The lack of oxygen was making me slow and disoriented. I forced myself to press on.

Remembering the blueprints, I positioned myself at the fourteenth panel from the right, very near the bottom of the *Sojourner*. This was the panel that held most of the wiring to the brig's electrical box. Or at least I thought it was.

243

38

**Now was the** tricky part.

I told the jet pack to hover and I looked around me. I planned the fastest way to get back to the *Spirit* and I held my breath.

This was it.

My plan was to just melt away the panel with the plasma torch and then melt all the exposed wires. It wasn't very precise, but it should work.

I flipped the torch on and immediately the metal hull began to melt away, exposing clumps of wires. I went at the wires with the torch and they quickly turned to sticky gobs of goo. I didn't know how many wires needed to be destroyed to kill the brig's power, and the fourteenth panel was insanely big. Like electri-bus big. I was really running out of time.

I looked at my oxygen gauge. It was blinking red and counting down from fifty-nine seconds.

"Crap!" I yelled, and instinctively looked around, expecting there to be an adult to yell at me. I laughed nervously.

"Dang!" I shouted, and I noticed that when I yelled, my oxygen rate didn't plummet quite as quickly.

"What's going on with the oxygen?" I asked out loud, and again I saw that the diminishing amount slowed. Then I remembered something about firefighters singing when they went into burning buildings. The singing helped conserve the air in their tanks. It was when they panicked and began breathing heavily that their oxygen disappeared quickly.

So I began to belt out the *MonsterMetalMachines* theme song while I nervously kept an eye on my gauge and tried to melt wires as fast as I could.

"Gimme iron, gimme steel!" I sang. "Gimme strength and an even keel!"

I remembered Mrs. H telling us never ever to shake a plasma torch, because of its instability. I shrugged and figured I had nothing to lose. I shook that thing like crazy, and just like I'd suspected, the plasma came shooting out ten times stronger. It was hard to control, but I held on as best I could.

"Moooonster. *MetalMachines*. Moooonster *MetalMachines*!"

I burned away more of the fourteenth panel's hull and went at the newly exposed wires. "We'll do anything to succeed! We fight to keep our spirits free!"

The now very unstable torch shot a stream of plasma about a hundred feet above my head and barely missed a porthole. I needed to turn this thing off before I breached the habitat layer. And I needed to get back to the *Spirit*. Now.

"Moooonster. *MetalMachines*. Moooonster *MetalMachines*!"

I immediately let go of the torch. I felt bad for littering space, but I couldn't bring an unstable plasma torch back with me on the ship. I was smart enough to know that. Larc would be proud.

I pushed away from the ship. "Moooonster. *MetalMachines*. Moooonster *MetalMachines*!"

My oxygen gauge began a warning countdown for the last ten seconds of air. I yelled, "Forward! Max speed!" and crossed my fingers.

"Three . . . two . . . one," the countdown blared in my ears.

"Moooonster. *MetalMachines*. Moooonster *MetalMachines*!"

39

**I was flying** so fast I almost overshot the flight deck capsule. Yelling, "Reverse immediately!" I slowed the jet pack just in time. With no oxygen left, and spots flashing before my eyes, I kicked the button to open the capsule hatch and clambered inside.

The hatch closed and I ripped my helmet off and threw it to the ground. I took huge gasping breaths and fell to my knees. After a moment I peeled the space suit off and left it in a clump on the floor.

My plan was to run to the nearest computer terminal. If I saw static from the brig camera, then I'd have proof the power was down and my mission was a success. I flew out of the flight deck, running at top speed. I rounded a corner and heard someone yell, "Here's one of 'em!"

Before I had a chance to reverse course, a stiff arm grabbed me by the front of the flight suit and roughly dragged me out into the lobby. I kicked and flailed and landed a nice loogie right in the guy's face but he still held on tight. He dragged me over to a bunch of other black-clad goons. I saw Meridiani, almost normal-sized, sitting on the floor with a boot-shaped bruise on his face.

I continued to fight and flail and I hollered that they'd never get away with this. I swear, if I ever read something like that in a book, I would think it was terribly cheesy. But it turns out you really do yell things like that when you're in trouble.

The goon gave me a swift slap in the face and it felt like fire. Wincing, I staggered back into the wall. I couldn't believe he actually hit me.

Grinding my teeth with rage, I lowered my still-pounding head and ran full tilt toward the thug's gut.

"Leave him alone!" a voice shouted from the distance. I stopped my attack to see who was yelling.

Dad!

"But, Dad, he *hit* me!" I protested.

"Not *you*, Michael. Him. You there!" Dad said, pointing at the man and walking briskly up to us. "Don't you ever, *ever* touch my son again." And with that, Dad slugged the dude right in the jaw. *My* jaw fell open. I couldn't believe Dad just hit that guy!

"Albert!" Mom's voice sounded distressed as she

came hurrying down the hall. Hubble was right behind her, as were lots of other people.

The goon looked like he was ready for a full-on throw-down with Dad, but luckily a couple of strong-looking guys from the crowd of *Spirit* and *Sojourner* folks came up and kept the goon from attacking.

With the *Spirit* and the *Sojourner* crews now combined, they easily outnumbered the Project goons.

"Mike!" Mom shouted from across the lobby. She charged toward me. Her nose was bloody and her flight suit was ripped, but she wore the biggest smile I'd ever seen.

"Mom!" I shouted. She bear-hugged me and I hugged her right back.

"Michael," she said, cupping my face, "where have you *been*?" She let go of my face and held me at arm's length while she looked me over.

"Nowhere, really . . . ," I said, and then the room tipped onto its side. I stumbled to catch my balance, expecting to see people flying everywhere. Did something just hit the ship? I didn't think these big ships could turn sideways!

"Michael!" Hubble shouted, running down the wall toward me. Then I realized that Hubble wasn't on the wall at all. Nothing was wrong with the ship. I was just extraordinarily dizzy.

"What have you been doing, Mr. Man?" Mom asked, her face swirling.

"Spacewalking," I mumbled.

"Mother of donkeys, Mike," Hubble said.

"I ran out of oxygen, after I melted the wires," I said, feeling very groggy.

"Melted the wires?" Mom looked incredulous. "Outside the ship?"

I nodded, watching black spots float in front of my eyes.

"We have to get him to the *Sojourner* sick bay," someone said in a faraway voice.

Another voice said, "Gather up the prisoners and get them onto the *Sojourner* as fast as you can."

I grabbed my head to try to stop the pounding.

"We need to abandon the *Spirit* and hop the next wormhole out of here," Mom said in slow motion. "A salvage crew can—"

The last thing I saw was a sideways view of Mom's boots and the dirty floor of the *Spirit*.

**40**

"**You have made** a terrible mistake," Mr. Shugabert growled.

My eyes flew open.

*Ugh.* I felt like I'd been run over by a truck. I lifted my head and zigzagging shots of pain exploded from eyeball to eyeball. The rest of me didn't feel great, either.

"You have started a war!" Shugabert's awful voice shouted.

Struggling through the pain, I sat up. Where was I? Did Sugar Bear have me at last?

"You'll never catch me!" I yelled at him. Or tried to yell. My voice came out slow and fuzzy, like Preditator when his batteries are running low.

I tried to jump out of bed and then realized I was tethered by an IV. What the . . . ?

A pair of hands grabbed my shoulders and gently pushed me back into a pile of pillows. "Calm down, snotdog. You're safe. It's just the viserator."

I was in a hospital room? On Earth? My eyes bugging, I looked down and saw that I was in my favorite *MonsterMetalMachines* T-shirt and boxers. Feeling terribly dizzy, but happy, I blinked a couple of times. As my eyes focused, I saw Stinky, Mom, Dad, Nita, and Hubble sitting at my bedside, watching the vis.

"Turn that irritating thing off," Mom commanded, and Nita switched off the vis. Sugar Bear's image, his hands and feet shackled, his face purple with rage as two police officers led him into a courthouse, flickered off.

"What?" I started. "What's going on?"

"You're home!" Stinky yelled gleefully, very gently socking me on the shoulder. "You're back! And you're a hero!"

I reached for the cup of water on a little table next to the bed. I swallowed a few sips and instantly felt refreshed.

"Added a little energy juju to that water," Dad said, motioning to my cup. "Ought to help you feel better pretty quickly."

"Thanks, Dad," I said. My voice was already less fuzzy and more normal.

"Yeah, you better thank me. You're being discharged

today. And if you're up for it, you're due back in school tomorrow morning."

"School! After all of this?" I was incredulous.

"You know how important a good education is, Mike," Mom said, ruffling my hair. "Plus, I managed to save your handheld for you. It looks like that report you were working on is finally done. Good job, Mr. Man."

I looked from person to person, in a state of shock. "School? I have to go back to school?"

"Get your naps in now, champ," Stinky said. "You've been laying around in this bed for four days. Mrs. H has a stack of homework for you that's taller than me."

I covered my face with my hands and tried to pass out again. No such luck.

**41**

"**When I woke** up this morning, I was nervous about finally giving my report." I cleared my throat. "I mean, I was all prepared and then I spent four days in the hospital hoping I didn't have brain damage." I smiled at my attempted joke and glanced at Mrs. H. She motioned for me to keep going.

"But here I go . . . and I want you to know, I've been researching this thing forever, so you better get comfortable."

I launched into my report, covering everything from mirror-sails to frankenbugs. I covered the Project and the recent moratorium on terraforming, enacted by the government until their investigation into Aurora Hazelwood is complete. I talked about how terraforming is, or was going to be, a *huge* business, and how

Aurora wanted to own a lot of companies that would help build colonies on terraformed planets, and how her dad said that was an ethical breach, and that was why she shipped him out to space and stranded him there by sending a virus to the plasma-propulsion units on the *Spirit*. I talked and talked until I needed some water. Then I talked some more.

I talked about the importance of proper research before jumping into something as complicated as terraforming. I talked about how if you terraform a planet too quickly, you can destroy it—just like what was happening to Aries. I talked about watchdog groups like the EFEs and how they're not lunatics, but an important part of society.

I kept talking until the other kids started eating their lunches at their desks. They were mesmerized by my presentation. They asked questions and I answered them. Mrs. H sat quietly at her desk, watching me with a sort of smile.

The amazing thing is that I slowly started to kind of have fun. I actually *liked* telling the class about what I'd learned. And I liked that they listened to me. And Stinky kept yelling things like "Don't forget to tell everybody that your parents eventually figured out the *Spirit* was out there the whole time, but Aurora had tried to bury that information!" and "How do you feel about your whole family being heroes for safely bringing the crews of *Spirit* and *Sojourner* home?" He was determined to make sure everyone understood that my parents were the good guys—and always had been. I was happy to let him interrupt. Mrs. H kept shaking her head, but she didn't stop him.

When I finally finished, I took a small silly bow and everyone clapped. I felt completely, utterly relieved. Not relieved to have my report finished, but relieved that everyone finally knew that my parents were heroes, not criminals. I hoped they all felt bad for how they treated me and my family. But schoolkids seemed petty after what I'd seen. . . . Marcy Fartsy is nothing compared to Mr. Shugabert.

After my bow I told the class that my report was dedicated to the world's only Liberation and Rescue Cyborg. Mrs. H smiled at that and I didn't even hear her face creak.

When the final bell rang, I gathered up my stuff.

"Come on," Stinky said, tugging my arm. "There's a *MonsterMetalMachines* marathon on channel 785. It starts in ten minutes. Hubble said he'd watch it with us."

We were about halfway to the door when the room darkened around us and that unmistakable smell of burnt coffee beans assaulted my nose. The tower of blue hair lunged in front of me and I stopped short.

"Mr. Stellar," Mrs. H said with her trademark sneer, "I wonder if you wouldn't join me for a minute?"

I hesitated, even though I knew she shouldn't be out to get me now. I took a deep breath and said to Stinky, "I'll meet you outside." Stinky bugged out his eyes as if to say "You're in trouble already?" and he walked quickly out the door.

I followed Mrs. H back to her desk.

"I know that you know I'm not really a teacher, Michael," she said, raising her eyes slowly to meet mine. I looked away out of habit.

"But nobody else knows that. The Project wants to keep my involvement in this whole . . . *fiasco* under wraps. I quite agree with them. That's why I'm here to finish out the school year. After this, though, I'm going back to my quiet retirement. And I don't want to be followed by viserator reporters; I don't want to write any books; and I don't want anyone to be able to find me."

I looked at her and nodded solemnly.

"Now, I know I've been tough on you, Michael. Sometimes you deserved it."

I gave a half smile.

She folded her arms across her chest and conceded, "Sometimes you didn't. And for that, I'm sorry. Initially I was excited by the proposition of a new search-and-rescue mission. But as the months wore on, I began to think your parents couldn't pull it off. I'm sorry for that, too. And I'm sorry for taking out my frustration with them on you."

257

I swallowed. I couldn't believe I was standing here with Venus Aldrin, Mrs. Halebopp, whoever . . . *apologizing* to me.

"Now," she said, regaining her stern, teacherly voice, "I understand it's customary for me to take a few days to grade big reports like this, but I wanted to go on and give you your grade now so that you can get started on your next assignment."

"Okay," I said, fearing what was about to come.

"Because you presented orally, I won't take points off for your use of first person. And your editorial comments were very relevant, considering the personal experiences you had regarding your subject. So other than speaking too softly at first, and then going on way too long . . . you did a pretty good job."

"P-p-pretty good?" I sputtered, not accustomed to compliments from her.

Mrs. Halebopp laughed. "You did a fine job, Mike. I give you an A."

I swallowed.

"An A, Mike. Did you hear me?"

"Sure. An A."

"You want a D instead?"

"No!" I said quickly. "I'm happy to have an A. I love A's! Thank you."

"Michael."

"Hmm?"

"Look at me. What's bothering you? You're not yourself. I'm not getting any smart-mouth comebacks. No excitement at all. What's the matter?"

I don't know why I opened up to her of all people . . . but I did. "I'm sad to have lost Larc. It's not fair to get Hubble back and lose someone else. Why did there have to be a trade-off? Why can't I have them both?"

"Oh, Michael, dear boy." Mrs. Halebopp hugged me. And though it should have been disgusting, it wasn't. "I know you miss her. I miss her, too."

Mrs. H reached into her desk and pulled out a disc for my handheld. "Before I say anything else, I want to give you this. It's your next assignment. I hope you do just as well on it."

A little confused about the abrupt change of subject, I took the disc. But before I could slide it into my handheld, she pulled something else out of her desk. It was a small metal box with a blinking blue light. She looked at it kind of . . . lovingly . . . and then handed it to me.

"What's this?" I asked, my voice barely above a whisper.

"Why don't you ask it?" she said with a twinkle in her eye.

I held the box up to the light and gave it a good once-over. It didn't look like anything special, just a shiny aluminum box about the size of my palm. But when I ran my hand over the blue light, the box spoke.

It said, "Space-time curvature!" in a very familiar voice.

"Larc?" I asked, furrowing my brow and shaking the box.

"Ack. Don't. Shake. Me."

Mrs. H laughed. "Now, don't get too excited, Mike. She obviously still has a long way to go. But in a few months Larc will be back in action. Only without the plasma-propulsion fuel cells this time."

"Yeah," the box said. "That sucked."

This time I laughed. "It really is you!"

"Well, technically, it's my central processor."

"Hubble managed to get it off the *Spirit*," Mrs. H said. "He didn't know if Jim would be able to reactivate it, but Jim's a genius."

"He sure is," I said.

"Genius. Genius. Genius," the box said.

"Speaking of genius," Mrs. H said, regaining her teacher voice, "I expect genius from you on your next project."

I slid the disc into my handheld. It said, "Please discuss, in detail, the principles behind travel through multiple dimensions." I furrowed my brow.

"Don't worry, Mike. I have a feeling you'll do just

fine. Besides, Larc is being reprogrammed to tutor students in dimensional travel."

"Quite a coincidence," I marveled, a smile growing on my face.

"Yes," Mrs. H answered with a sly grin. "Quite."

"What's happening?" the box asked. "I can't see a thing."

We laughed. Then Mrs. H reached out her hand. "For now, though, Mike, I'm going to need the box back. Jim needs it for programming. But you're welcome to visit him anytime you want."

I handed the box back and said, "Sure. That would be great. Hey, Larc, I'm going airboarding at your *nanny's* park this weekend."

"My nanny!" said Larc, with a great hee-haw.

"And, Mike," Mrs. Halebopp said, standing up from her desk and walking me to the classroom door, "the new teacher will expect your dimensional travel report immediately after the three-week summer break. Barring any crazed executive assistant spies, intra-universal space-walking sickness, or escape pod hijackings, I would expect you to get it turned in on time."

I chuckled as I stood by the classroom door, happy to feel a breeze ruffle my hair. I realized I wasn't bothered by the burnt coffee bean smell. I smiled. Mrs. H gave me a long look with her not-quite-so-scary beetle-black eyes.

And then she winked. It was a creak-free wink, and it didn't creep me out at all. I waved bye to Mrs. H and jogged over to Stinky.

"Hurry up!" Stinky said, walking briskly down the sidewalk and shouting at me over his shoulder. "Preditator ate ScoopaZoid five minutes ago. Hubble just called on the peapod. *Come on* before we miss the whole thing!"

"Okay, okay, you fart on a stick, I'm coming." I ran past him and whacked him on the arm. "Last one there has to sit between the lovebirds. *Moooonster-MetalMachines* . . ."